T0265587

Violin-Making
a practical guide

Juliet Barker

THE CROWOOD PRESS

First published in 2001 by
The Crowood Press Ltd
Ramsbury, Marlborough
Wiltshire SN8 2HR

enquiries@crowood.com

www.crowood.com

Paperback edition 2022

© Juliet Barker 2001

All rights reserved. No part of this publication may be reproduced or
transmitted in any form or by any means, electronic or mechanical,
including photocopy, recording, or any information storage and retrieval
system, without permission in writing from the publishers.

British Library Cataloguing-in-Publication Data
A catalogue record for this book is available from the British Library.

ISBN 978 0 7198 4133 0

Line drawings by Rebecca Downing

Typeset by Textype Typesetters

Cover design by Maggie Mellett

Printed and bound in Great Britain by CPI Group (UK) Ltd, Croydon

CONTENTS

LIST OF ILLUSTRATIONS

PREFACE

This book was written with amateur violin-makers in mind, but I hope that it will also interest student violin-makers, and even more experienced ones. I have learned a great deal from the professional makers who have come to help with teaching the weekly amateur classes and summer residential courses we run in our workshop, and from my pupils; indeed, I have also learned from pupils that it is not always the best made instruments that sound best, but often a first instrument does. There are several possible explanations for this, and I hope that this fact will encourage those contemplating making their first instrument.

The traditional methods of making I was taught in Mittenwald would have had their roots in the ways of Füssen, where most of the early makers came from. I believe that my teachers, including one named Mathias Klotz (a direct descendent of the Mathias Klotz who first made violins in Mittenwald around 1675), had all made violins for a living before they came to teach us and were paid by the instrument rather than the hour. The methods they used were the fastest possible and therefore also the easiest. I too have tried to describe the easiest way to make a violin, a viola or a cello, for the methods are similar – only the size is different. Describing actions in words is not easy, especially after forty years of demonstrating things as I taught people. Please always read through a whole chapter and then go back to its beginning. It is easier to understand what you are to do if you have an idea of what it is that you are aiming for.

I have tried to keep the number of tools required to the minimum and I have described ones that an amateur should be able to make; some readers will probably already have a more comprehensive set of tools. I have, for example, a half-round hand-cut rasp. It is an expensive tool but it can be used where I describe the use of a 'file' in the text for such things as shaping end blocks, making the outline of the scroll and even for finishing the neck. But I do not use it often for I dislike the noise it makes. Violin-making should be a quiet occupation. It is also one that, even after nearly fifty years, I still find enthralling. Although I have enjoyed writing this book, the great joy of finishing it is that I shall now have more time to make. One of the pleasures of making a violin is that the result shows off the beauty of the wood from which it was made. Take pleasure in using that wonderful, natural material, love your tools, care for them well and enjoy violin-making.

ACKNOWLEDGEMENTS

I am most grateful to the Commune di Cremona for permission to include photographs taken by Linea Tre of their Andrea Amati violin; to Philip Mynott for the cover photographs and a dozen of those in the book; to Bernard Michaud for the photographs of the fine spruce tree and sawing a log, and to James Beament for endless patience while taking all the rest. Several of the diagrams are copied from those drawn by Mick Nelson in 1978 for our first summer school and I thank him for permission to use them. I must thank Rebecca Downing for taking great trouble in drawing the diagrams exactly as I wanted them, and persevering patiently until they were completed.

I thank Charles Beare for correcting some errors in my draft of the first chapter; Quentin Playfair for ideas, encouragement and one or two sentences; all the pupils who have inadvertently helped me assemble the material in the book, and two who have wittingly helped: Fleur d'Antal for helping to clarify the meaning and my English, and, most particularly, Marjorie Winter who has word-processed the text and made many helpful suggestions and emendations, remaining cheerful even when I said for the fifth time 'maybe we could put this sentence in there'.

I must particularly give warm thanks to the Crowood Press who have been most helpful, giving clear advice and encouragement when I felt discouraged, and to David Dyke for suggesting my name to them in the first place. It caused me to sit down and write a book that had been incubating since 1964, the year before our first son Tom was born; perhaps I should thank him for preventing me from writing the book too soon. I must certainly thank our younger son Christopher Beament for helping me to obtain time free from teaching for writing and reading, for making suggestions and, in particular, for allowing me to quote long sections of his excellent varnishing guide, written for our pupils.

Most of all, I must thank my husband James Beament, whose encyclopaedic knowledge has answered my questions, who has acted as skilled photographer, patient secretary and general adviser and has been entirely supportive throughout.

J.B.
Cambridge
January 2001

1 A SHORT HISTORY OF VIOLIN-MAKING

Today, at the beginning of the twenty-first century, there are violin-making schools all over the world, Chinese and American pupils study in Italy, Canadians and Germans come to England. France, Japan, America and Germany all have their own schools. Violin-making has become globalized. Though the instruments of one maker are sometimes recognizable, it is no longer possible to look at a violin and say whether it is French or Italian, or from any other particular country. National characteristics have disappeared.

What was the situation 500 years ago? Musical instruments had already been made for a long time and man first used horsehair to bow a string more than 500 years earlier somewhere in the Middle East. From there stringed instruments spread into Europe, north into the Balkans and south with the expansion of Islam into north Africa, Sicily, Italy and Spain. They were carried by wandering peoples such as Sephardic Jews, who moved south from the Middle East to Morocco, then to Spain and were later driven by religious persecution to north Italy and, by 1550, as far as England. They would have had with them not only uds, forerunners of the lute, but also rebecs, the ancestors of the violin. A rebec had a back hollowed out from a solid piece of wood which extended to make the neck and the pegbox, and a flat top which had to support a bridge. It also had a fingerboard which projected above the front, an important improvement in

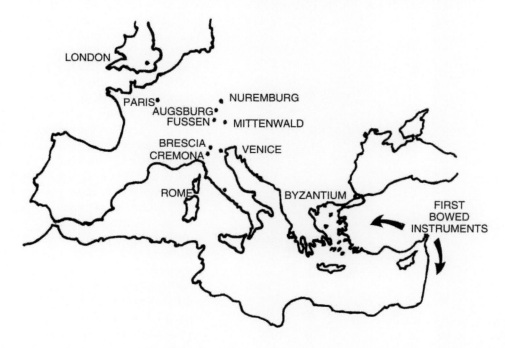

A map of the main places involved in the development of the violin.

design, releasing the front from the downward leverage of the fingerboard pulled by the strings and leaving the front free to vibrate. Viols developed from early guitar-like instruments. The early fiddle took the ribs of guitars glued on to the carved back of a rebec and eventually added a carved front, a fretless neck and a scroll with three, four or even five pegs. By 1300 there were folk fiddles all over Europe, played up on the shoulder rather than held between the knees like the viol, and tuned in fifths – loud, cheerful instruments for dancing that would have been made to various designs.

There were good trade routes in Europe, first built by the Romans and then kept useable through the Middle Ages. Not only traders and wandering musicians travelled these roads, but also apprentices, who, when they had worked for four or five years for their masters, became journeymen and went to work for other masters, taking their skills with them and learning new ones and designs too. One main route from Venice to Augsburg and on to Flanders passed through Füssen in the Tyrol, where the Emperor Maximilian I kept one of his courts at the beginning of the sixteenth century. He employed many musicians and the instrument makers flourished there, as the wood they needed grew just up the mountainside. By then makers knew that spruce made the best soundboards or fronts for stringed instruments and they often used figured maple for the ribs, backs, heads and necks. Both these woods are common near Füssen, and, as the town was also a trading centre, they would have sold wood north to Nuremberg and the Netherlands and south to Venice, the great distribution centre of spices, silks and resins from the east, wool and leather from the north, and wood coming from the West Alps in France to the East Alps in Austria and beyond.

Probably the first recognizable violin was made near Milan and then developed further in Cremona and then Brescia. It is interesting that it flourished first in city-republics and not at the courts of dukes or princes, where the nobles had a refined and conservative taste for the gentler viol. The earliest violins that still exist today in their miraculous beauty are those of Andrea Amati of Cremona. Most famous is the set of instruments ordered by Charles IX of France, probably at the suggestion of his mother Catherine of Medici. That these instruments were ordered around 1560 must have meant that Amati, who was born at the beginning of that century, was already famous as a violin, viola and cello maker. He made small violins and ones similar to the standard violin as we know it, alto and tenor violas – today violas are still not standard-sized – and large cellos. Also famous in Europe were the tenor violas of Gasparo da Salo, a maker thirty-five years younger than Amati, who worked in Brescia, a town in the Venetian Republic. As the instruments were distributed across Europe, makers further afield would have

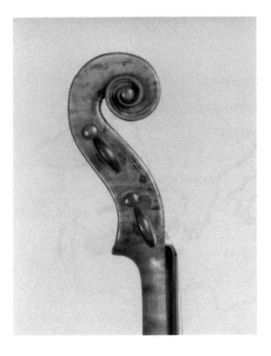

Scroll of the violin made by Andrea Amati in 1566 for Charles IX of France [property of Cremona City Council].

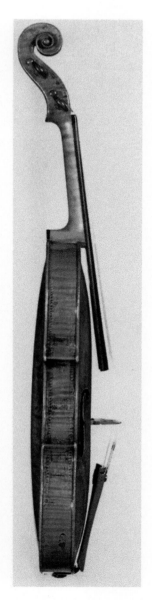

seen them and begun to make instruments of the violin family as well as viols and would have modified the designs to their own taste.

But from Cremona and Brescia came the two most influential designs. Gasparo da Salo's style was carried on by his pupil Maggini and much later influenced Guarnerius del Gesu. The Amati style descended through his family to Nicolo Amati, the one violin-maker who survived the plague in Cremona, who taught Andrea Guarnerius, the first member of that violin-making family, and probably Stradivarius too. In 1700 Stradivarius at fifty-six was a flourishing maker, the Austrian Jacob Stainer, a maker influenced by the Amatis and Nicolo Amati himself, had been dead for over fifteen years, Guarnerius del Gesu had just been born.

LEFT: *Back of the Andrea Amati violin.*

MIDDLE: *Front of the Andrea Amati violin.*

ABOVE: *Side view of the Andrea Amati violin.*

These makers have had the greatest influence on all subsequent violin-making.

Over the next hundred years there was no radical change in design, although gradually as the fashion for Italian art and music declined, each European country further developed its own style of music and violin-making. The guild system of apprenticeship was still the way to learn a trade, but as the number of makers increased, journeymen would have wandered less far and small differences in working methods could show in which city or area an instrument had been made. There were, for instance, many different ways of fixing a neck into or onto a violin body. There is no standard baroque method. To generalise, the designs in northern Europe were influenced by Stainer and Amati, but further south in Italy makers used a Stradivarius-inspired pattern.

As the power of wind and brass instruments increased, violins needed to be louder and the popularity of the higher arched Amati and Stainer pattern violins declined and makers turned to Stradivarius and later Guarnerius del Gesu models. Many old violins were given longer necks set at a greater angle and stronger and longer bass-bars, so, while string tensions were greater, the violin fronts could withstand the increased pressure. The manufacturing of strings had also improved so the core of the string could be thinner and the weight increased by adding more metal winding, thereby allowing the tension to be increased. Necks were cut away more near the violin body so that players could reach higher notes with greater comfort. The possibility of using a bridge with a greater curvature at the top ensured that strong bowing did not make two strings vibrate at once, though it also made the playing of chords more difficult.

In the middle of the eighteenth century piecework was already beginning.

Production was speeded up if one man made only scrolls, another only bodies and yet another assembled the parts and handed them on to be varnished and set up. The firm of Neuner and Hornsteiner practised the method in Mittenwald, and it was used in Markneukirchen, also in Germany, and later Mirecourt in France. The workmanship is good although lacking in individuality, but these violins could satisfy the demands of the professional players, amateurs and students who came from the new music schools which opened first in Paris just before 1800, followed by several in Germany.

Those players who could afford to would have patronized the master violin makers who continued to work all over Europe. The wealthiest players would have looked for old instruments with famous names on their labels. Vuillaume in Paris encouraged this trade, but as early as 1676 Thomas Mace wrote, 'We chiefly value old instruments before new, for by experience they are found to be by far the best.' This desire has led many makers to try to make their new instruments look old. Of all orchestral instruments only the strings have this problem, that old instruments are preferred to new, as wind and brass instruments continue to develop and their players usually prefer new instruments, and, unlike stringed instruments, old wind and brass instruments cannot be tuned to today's pitch. The small changes in violin design have followed the needs of the music written for the instrument, and the first design was remarkably good. Now there is nothing more that can be changed. A violin is a violin, and contemporary composers love it or leave it.

Modern makers have the opportunity to look at some of the best instruments of the last 450 years and to see the work of their peers. Fifty years ago there were few makers and violin-making seemed a dying trade. Today there are many makers, and both their skill and the competition to succeed are great.

Mass-produced violins are still made in a few eastern European countries and particularly in China, where there are also skilled makers. The cheap factory instruments in all sizes are heavy and difficult to play and it is not surprising that some of the children who are provided with them give up playing. Here particularly is an opening for amateur makers. Good small violins, violas and cellos are rare, and, although carefully made new ones can have a remarkably good tone for their size, making them is not commercially viable.

As for the professional makers, they will continue to make accurate copies, free interpretations of classical instruments or original designs. With luck those who buy them will become less prejudiced in favour of old instruments and realize that tone depends not only on the instrument but also on the ears and hands of the player.

2 DESIGN

Geometry in 1500 was taught in Italian universities and in the schools at ducal courts where gifted poor boys were educated, as well as the sons of the nobility. Artisans would have known some arithmetic and could often read enough to follow instructions but were unlikely to know the theory of the golden section on which so many Renaissance designs were based. However, they would have been aware of it and they would have had compasses and ruler; and a violin is an assembly of beautiful curves which has evolved because of the needs of the player. Most of the basic, practical problems of instrument design had already been resolved by the makers and players of the violin's antecedents.

The player nowadays expects the correct proportion of neck length to body stop and bridge position which, in turn, fixes the position of the f-holes. For anyone wishing to design an original instrument – and it is better to have made one or two on classical patterns first – the placing of the bridge is the starting point, followed by the f-holes and their relationship to the middle bout or C-curve. This must not be so wide that it gets

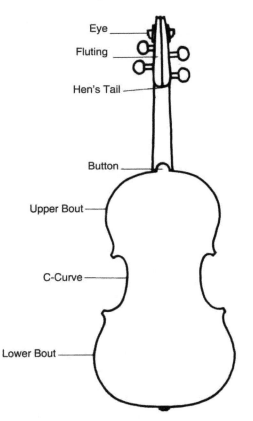

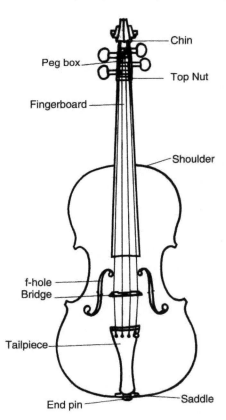

The back of a violin with the names of its parts.

RIGHT: The front of a violin with the names of its parts.

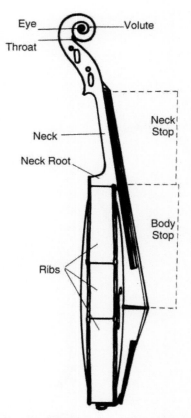

Eye — Volute

Throat

Neck

Neck Root

Ribs

Neck Stop

Body Stop

LEFT: The side of a violin with the names of its parts.

giving most of the necessary information and also plans available from museums. For those who do not wish to copy a classical violin there are workshop patterns on which makers can impose archings and corners to taste, though the three basic templates for outline, scroll and f-holes must have similar curves and, to a certain extent, the outline generates the arching curve.

Violas may be more experimental in design since they are made, not only with different body lengths, but also with string lengths varying greatly in proportion to body length. Players will be happier if the neck is in proportion to the body stop and if the shoulders are sloping to facilitate shifts into higher positions. For power, f-holes set further apart would seem to be better although again there are exceptions. If anyone considers making a five-string, violin-cum-viola he has the insoluble problem that a five-string bridge needs greater width, but for the player to bow five strings separately the waist of the instrument must be narrower. Alternatively, the bridge could be higher, but this is undesirable as it would still further increase the pressure on the bridge beyond that already added by the extra string. Innovation is problematic.

Cellos have evolved with ribs nearly twice as high proportional to their body length as violins. This has resulted in the distance from the front of the cello up to the fingerboard being greater. If it were not, the player would bump the shoulder of the instrument when trying to shift to higher positions. With the added difference of playing a cello downwards rather than its being held on the shoulder, cellists prefer a ratio of 7:10 for the neck length to body stop rather than that of 2:3 expected by violinists.

Always remember that the practical needs of the player are more important than the sheer beauty of the design – though luckily the two often go together.

in the way of the bow. The C-curve also supports the arch of the back and the front, so the practical demands of the player led to a practical design. The arching itself is necessary to withstand the pressure the strings put on the bridge. That the design of the violin is impossible to improve on is proved by the fact that it has remained virtually unchanged since 1550. A trained eye can detect difference of outline, f-holes, corners, archings and scrolls, but to many players a violin is a tool. Theoretically a flatter arching, for example, should lead to a violin with a more powerful tone, but there are so many exceptions to any possible theory that it seems best just to aim for smoothly flowing curves and follow traditional wisdom.

Not many makers have access to a good classical violin from which to take templates, but there are well-drawn posters

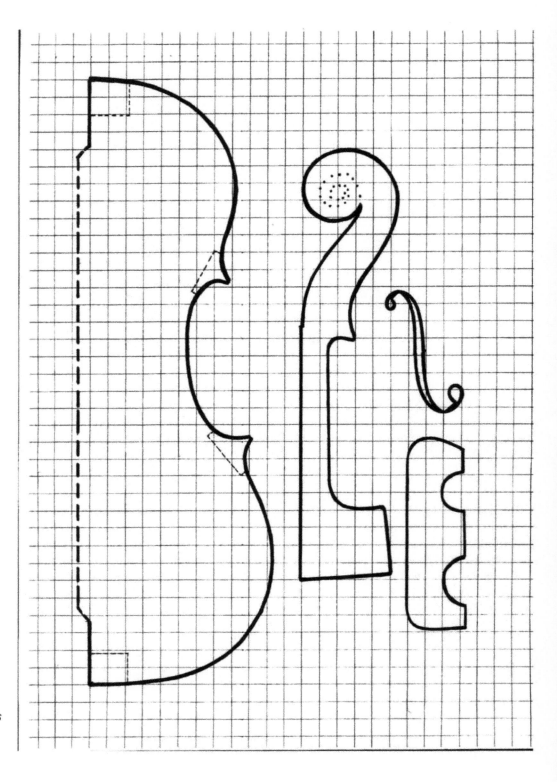

Workshop violin templates drawn on 10mm squares and reduced.

3 MATERIALS

WOOD

Choosing the wood for an instrument is most important since the tone will depend to a great extent on the wood. Timber may be quarter sawn or slab cut.

In violin-making spruce, a soft wood, is always quarter sawn, but the hard wood may be sawn either way. All wood is more stable if quarter sawn and so is preferable for necks and ribs, but slab wood may also be used. It is more flexible and particularly suitable for viola backs. However, the real essential for all instruments is good spruce. Each dark grain line is autumnal growth when the tree, anticipating winter gales, puts in more lignin, which is strong.

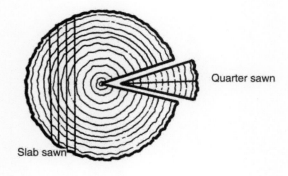

Quarter sawn

Slab sawn

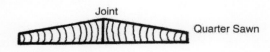

Joint

Quarter Sawn

ABOVE: View from above a tree trunk showing the different directions in which it can be sawn.

FAR LEFT: A fine spruce tree showing clearly the first 5ms which Le Bois de Lutherie later cut for instrument fronts.

Bernard Michaud sawing a quarter of a maple tree trunk into wedges for cello backs at Le Bois de Lutherie.

View from above of a 'tree trunk' made from wedges, with two halves of a back and front taken out and glued on to the adjacent halves.

In between is the faster growing spring wood containing more cellulose, which is softer. Violin-makers look for fine autumn growth rings. When cutting curves that cross the grain at a slight angle it is difficult to cope with a strong, wide grain, especially if there is a wide, soft spring growth between them. Evenness of grain does not affect the tonal quality of the wood. Much more important is how the wood splits. Ideally, each log of violin length is split through the centre into quarters and then sawn into wedges. Splitting wood is not as economical as sawing but it shows the qualities and problems such as twist. Trees growing on a slope or in a windy place are prone to this and their wood is more difficult to work, and, if the wood is sawn, its problems are more difficult to detect. When looking at wedges of sawn spruce, if the two edges that will be glued together are fairly smooth it is possible to see little flecks that follow the line of how the wood will split and these should be as parallel to the sawn faces as possible.

If the flecks are also parallel to these

RIGHT: The edges of a spruce wedge, planed and showing the little resin lines that indicate how the wood will split.

faces on the thinner edge of the wedge, the wood is good. Also, on both spruce and maple look for grain lines that are parallel to the edge along the face next to the thick edge of the wedges that will be joined. The joint will then be easier to make and will be more stable. Very fine grained spruce can be weak, and I would choose wood with fewer than eight grain lines to a centimetre.

Spruce trees have mechanisms for letting all their sap drain away in the winter and so they can grow at higher altitudes than broadleaved trees. Spruce is a remarkable wood. It was used for aircraft frames and for the ratio of its lengthwise strength to its weight there is still no stronger material. The speed of sound along the grain is approximately twice as fast as that across the grain, it is very elastic and yet has good damping. It is, as was discovered hundreds of years ago, ideal for soundboards, curved or flat, for keyboards and for plucked and bowed instruments. But bear in mind that the most expensive wood is not always best for tone; always choose lightweight spruce.

Maple is ideal for backs, ribs and scrolls. Though less elastic than spruce, it is stronger and also splits well and makes a good box on to which to glue the spruce front. Figured maple is preferred by violin-makers as it is pretty. Figuring is a slight genetic modification that occurs in many woods. If such a timber is split, it has a corrugated surface at an angle to the grain and, when this is planed smooth, the light is reflected differently by the tops, sides and bottoms of the waves. The deeper the waves, the greater is the ripple effect in the wood and the more difficult it is to work. Unfigured maple is used for bridges. In all timbers there are medullary rays which carry sap from the bark of the tree towards the centre; they run more or less parallel to the figure at right angles to the grain lines. Maple with strongly marked rays is chosen for bridges as it is less likely to break than figured maple.

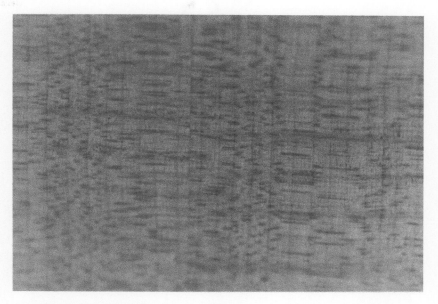

Other timbers that may be used for backs, ribs and scrolls and are sometimes figured are poplar or alder (which are more open grained and therefore difficult to make smooth by using traditional

A piece of maple suitable for bridges, magnified to show medullary rays, and also how invisible a good joint should be.

Wood for a violin, showing the figure of the maple angled towards the join, and the grain lines of the spruce parallel to it.

Varieties of Wood				
English	**French**	**German**	**Latin**	**Specific Gravity**
maple	érable	Ahorn	Acer campestre/plantanoides	0.65
spruce	sapin	Fichte	Picea abies/excelsa	0.4
ebony	ébène	Ebenholz	Diospyrus ebenum (Sri Lanka)	1.09
			Diospyrus crassifolia (Africa)	1.03
box	buis	Buxbaum	Buxus sempervirens	0.91
rosewood	palisandre	Palisander	Dalbergia nigra (Brazil)	0.85
			Dalbergia latifolia (East Indies)	0.85
holly	houx	Stechpalme	Ilex aquifolium	0.8
hornbeam	charme	Hainbuche	Carpinus betulus	0.75
beech	hêtre	Buche	Fagus sylvatica	0.72
apple	pommier	Apfelbaum	Malus sylvestris	0.71
pear	poirier	Birnbaum	Pyrus communis	0.70
cherry	cerisier	Kirschbaum	Prunus avium	0.61
lime	tilleul	Linde	Tilea vulgaris/europaea	0.54
alder	aune	Erle	Alnus glutinosa	0.53
poplar	peuplier	Pappel	Populus nigra	0.45
willow	saule	Weide	Salix alba	0.4

tools), beech or hornbeam (which are tough) and several fruit woods, cherry being particularly good; but it is difficult to beat the maple family. Softwood seasons quickly and spruce which is two years old may be used, while maple should have dried in wedges for at least four years.

For linings and blocks any lightweight wood that splits straight may be used, though woodworm does like willow and alder. However, if a violin is played woodworm will not attack it. Pessimists may always use cedar.

Ebony is usual for fingerboards and tailpieces. It can be polished to a fine surface and is dense and hard. It is also used for pegs, which can also be made from box or rosewood. Those who do not want to use tropical hardwoods may replace them with holly or box, but these are not as durable.

The traditional woods are best, and spruce is essential for the front of any member of the violin family. Small-sized instruments may have backs and ribs made from lighter, more flexible woods and so can violas.

The specific gravity of any type of wood may vary considerably from one plank to another and little of the ebony we use sinks in water, so that our figure for ebony should be nearer 0.95 though the best could be 1.03.

GLUE

The best glue for violin-making is hide glue made from the rejected scrapings and thinnings from leather factories. These are limed to change insoluble collagen into soluble protein. The lime is then neutralized with acid and the remaining mixture is thoroughly washed. It is gradually dried and formed into sheets or crystals with a small amount of preservative added. Glue is best prepared in an old mug or a jam jar with a nylon line across the top to wipe the brush on, and a lid should be provided. Metal glue pots are unsuitable because they turn the glue black. The glue should be soaked in twice its volume of water for an hour or two. It should be stirred during the first few minutes until each piece has absorbed enough water not to stick to the others. Then it should be heated in a water bath at a temperature of 50–60°C. The jam jar is less likely to crack if it is sitting on a piece of wood in the saucepan. If the water gets too hot, the glue denatures and does not bond so well. Regularly heated glue will last for days, but if it goes at all mouldy it should be thrown away.

The big advantage of hide glue is that it glues to itself. If a joint glued with casein or synthetic glue opens, all the adhesive has to be removed before a new application may be made. If a joint glued with hide glue opens, more glue can be worked into the joint and it can be recramped successfully. However, any thickness of hide glue is weak. It is not a strong substance in itself and only provides a good bond between two well-fitting pieces of wood. It is strong under tension but will break if subjected to a shock. This has the advantage that, if an instrument is dropped, the glue should break before the wood does, but it also means that a violin-maker, unlike a wood-carver, can never use a mallet on a chisel.

Porous woods such as alder or spruce absorb more glue and bond more strongly than other woods. Some hard pieces of maple may be difficult to join permanently, and if, when gouged across the grain, the shavings break on the centre join it is wise to rub in a little thin glue each time a new surface of the joint is exposed.

TOOLS

All violin-makers have tools that they love and would not be without; and even a machine or two may be useful, particularly a bandsaw, a bench drill and a grindstone. The list below is as short as it is reasonable to make it. Violins have been made with little more than a penknife but it is easier with more tools and those with money can buy almost all while those with time can make several.

In Mittenwald, where traditions change slowly, the violin-makers use knives, planes and chisels, seldom rasps or files and their traditional methods of working are similar to those used in most of Europe centuries earlier. Years ago rasps and files were tools that would have been expensive and not easily sharpened so a poor wood-worker used them as little as possible. This choice of tools has great advantages. Now as then, a sharp knife in skilled hands can cut swinging, elegant curves better than any other tool, and if the bevels, on which it is sharpened, are kept really flat, knives are not difficult to control. Sharpening any tool on a straight bevel makes its use easier. Violin-makers do not use mallets and so can sharpen to a fine edge angled as low as 23 degrees. This is especially desirable on the gouge that will be used on the fluting of the purfling, for example, this leaves a long surface to push down on, which helps in controlling the tool. A gouge can be used like a low-angled plane.

A flat surface is necessary: part of the slate bed of a pool-table, a piece of marble, well-supported float-glass or even a good quality piece of blockboard. This may be rubbed with graphite and will show up the high spots on any piece of wood tested on it.

Tools to be bought, new or old:
- No. 9½ block plane, for many jobs from surfacing and thicknessing ribs to planing fingerboards.
- Longer jack plane, around 18in for joints and flattening surfaces.
- Square, higher than the rib height of the instrument being made.
- 12in (300mm) rule with millimetres on

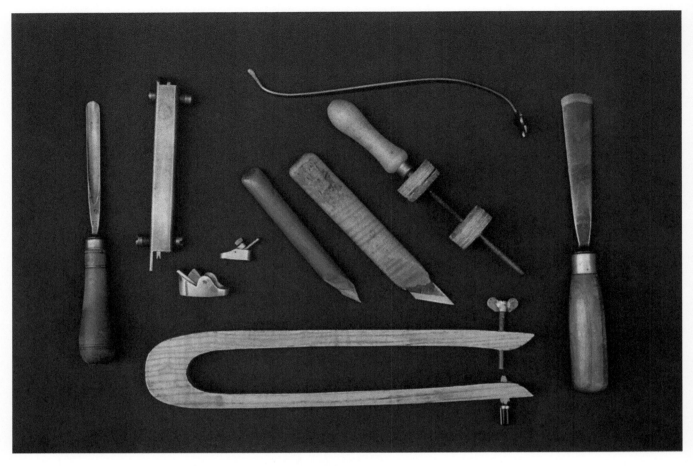

A selection of favourite tools, one-third actual size.

both sides of one face; if sturdy this will double as a straight edge.

- Small hammer for pressing in purfling, adjusting small planes and even getting the mould out.
- Hand drill with 6mm and 1.5mm bits for pegholes and holes in pegs.
- Dividers: useful for marking string widths at nut and bridge.
- Pencil compasses for checking the symmetry of measurements.
- Narrow, accurate, metal tape-measure.
- Small marking/cutting gauge which can be made to take a pencil as well.
- Vernier or dial calliper for checking thicknesses.
- Small back saw or Exacto saw mainly

for use on the scroll.
- Coping saw for rough outlines.
- Fret saw for making patterns and cutting f-holes.
- 1mm-thick cabinet scraper for finishing difficult ribs.
- Sheet of 0.3mm steel for making scrapers; tough tin snips for cutting these out will be needed.
- Flat chisel, 7mm wide, for peg-box and scroll bevels.
- Flat chisel, 18mm wide, for setting necks and shaping blocks.

Straight gouges:
- 30mm No. 4 for rough arching.
- 20mm No. 5 mainly for carving the scroll.
- 15mm No. 6 mainly for carving the scroll.

- 10mm No. 7 for gouging round the purfling and carving the scroll.
- 6mm No. 8 for the eye of the scroll.
- Inside ground 18mm No. 6 (for instance, an old turning chisel) for shaping the corner blocks.

   Sharp tools are safer than blunt ones and are a pleasure to use.

- Combination waterstone 1000/6000 grit or similar.
- Sharpening cone.
- At least three F-cramps or similar, 50mm depth, 150mm minimum length.
- Stiff-bladed craft knife for cutting round the purfling, the ends of soundposts and even f-holes.
- Flat file length of cut 200mm cut 0 medium.
- Crossing file length of cut 150 mm cut 0 medium.
- Flat file length of cut 75mm cut 0 medium.
- Half-round needle file 5mm wide at least 100mm length of cut.
- Needle file with fine point for bridge and nut grooves.
- Square-bladed bradawl for marking holes and beginning f-holes.
- Peg-hole reamer which can be used to make a peg shaper.
- Two knife blades, 18mm, 10mm or complete knives; the violin-maker's best tool for cutting curves and trimming purfling.
- Steel table knife (with a thin blade; may be found in junk shops).
- Thirty-six or so wooden clothes pegs, sawn short and with strong springs.
- Sandpaper, when it is referred to, refers to abrasive paper in general, such as garnet or aluminium oxide, and assumes three grades: 180 grit, 240 grit and 320 grit; it works best if made into neat strips and folded into three; it has a tendency to round surfaces and so is of limited use; the dried skin of a small dogfish may be used (if each piece is checked for points which might cause scratches) and also the dried stalks of mares' tails; before using either dogfish or mares' tails soak them in water and then dry them on a cloth.

Tools to buy or make:
- Two small, round soled planes, 24mm and 36mm overall length; if making wooden ones, make the mouth first.
- Bevel: simple to make from two pieces of wood, a metal screw and a butterfly nut.
- Purfling marker: this tool comes in many designs; two blades are held parallel to a leg which follows one or both edges of the violin.
- Purfling pick.
- Closing cramps can be made from lengths of 5mm studding with one end in a handle and two 20mm-wide wooden washers covered with cork, leather or soft plastic, with a nut embedded in one.
- Sound post setter.
- A dental mirror (ask your dentist for one); give it a wooden handle.
- Bending iron; instructions are given in the text.
- Pencil calliper, as in the photograph.
- Point calliper as used by Stradivarius.
- Peg shaper; a block of wood 100mm long, 50mm wide (70mm for cellos), with a hole drilled 30mm in from each end and reamed, one larger, one smaller and then steps cut to take blades.

A point calliper similar to one used by Stradivarius for thicknessing.

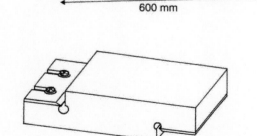

Butterfly nuts

150 mm

Hinge

600 mm

Side view of a peg shaper.

*Useful shapes for a
set of scrapers;
actual size.*

- Set of scrapers.
- Bass-bar cramps.
- Cradle: either just a rim support, known as a danger board, or a piece of 25mm deal or chipboard hollowed out to the inverse shape of the arching and lined with carpet underlay or similar soft, non-slip material.
- Fingerboard cradle; similarly, the inverse of the fingerboard curve.
- Bridge cradle.
- Cramping blocks of many sorts.

4 THE RIB STRUCTURE

TEMPLATE

There are many ways of making a violin but the easiest if not the most accurate is on an inside mould. To make a mould a template is necessary; 1.5mm plywood is the best material to use but aluminium will do or even plastic. Many plans come with a rib line drawn as well as an outline; if not, or if copying a particular instrument, create an inside rib line allowing for its overhang and the rib thickness and remembering that the overhang at the corners is usually greater. If copying a drawing of a given template, remember that the new template must fit inside the drawn line otherwise outlines and scrolls get bigger and f-holes smaller. Unless making an asymmetric outline only a half template is used and it must be the shape of the inside of the ribs.

MOULD

For the mould take a piece of plywood about one-third the height of the ribs; for cellos use two pieces of 25mm blockboard with spacers

- where the heads of the cramps will come;
- at the block recesses; and
- the four extremities.

Draw a centreline and then draw round the template on both sides and mark the block recesses. These are marked on the workshop template and can be scaled up or down for different sizes of instrument. The mould is cut out and machined or rasped to the exact shape. Keep the edges square. The middle of the mould is removed to receive the heads of the cramps which will later be used to hold in place the rib-cramping blocks.

THE BLOCKS

The blocks are easier to shape if the wood – spruce, lime, willow or any lightweight wood – splits at right angles to the base. So first split the block of wood across the grain; plane this surface smooth as it will be the face that glues to the mould.

Then plane the base at right angles to this face and at right angles to the grain lines. At this stage it is as well to leave the blocks 1.5mm higher than the eventual rib heights.

It is easier to plane the corner blocks in pairs and split them apart only when they are to the appropriate height. Probably the early makers, and certainly Stradivarius, set the neck into the ribs before gluing on the back and the front, and, when they planed the projecting neck root at the top block, they made it lower than the bottom one. They may also have done this for aesthetic reasons; looking at a violin from the side, with a larger lower curve and a narrower upper curve, if the ribs were parallel they would look as though they widened. Aim for a flat taper unless you have good reason to do otherwise.

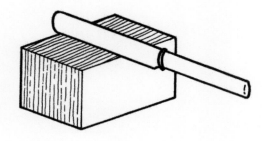

Using a table knife to split block wood.

Planing the end of a piece of block wood.

Place the mould on two supporting strips of plywood slightly thicker than the mould, on a flat surface and apply a little glue to the long edge of the recesses and the matching surface of the blocks, being careful not to get glue in the corners or on the sides of the recesses. Ensure that the bases of the blocks are sitting on the flat surface.

Always wipe off any visible glue; soft glue is easy to remove, hard glue is not.

RIBS

Decide how the rib figure will relate to the back, either as in the diagram opposite or with all the figure at the same angle or random. Flatten the outside face of each rib by removing as little wood as possible and finish to a smooth surface with a plane and, if necessary, a cabinet scraper. Plane the other side to a uniform thickness of 1mm for violins and violas and 1.4mm for cellos.

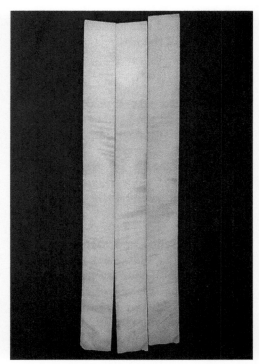

LEFT: *A completed mould with blocks.*

RIGHT: *Three pretty ribs laid side by side, matching the figure.*

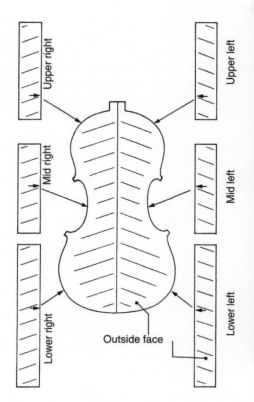

LEFT: Deciding how the figure of the ribs should follow on from the figure of the back.

Checking the thickness of ribs.

Ribs should be cut to generous lengths, allowing at least 10mm extra. Sometimes backs come with three ribs, sometimes more. They are rarely long enough for two lower ribs to come out of one length, although, if they are, consider having one continuous piece for both lower ribs. Usually they are long enough for a lower and an upper rib or three mid ribs. If they are long enough only for a lower and a mid rib or two uppers, I still think it best to cut all the ribs to length. The mid ribs are most likely to break when bending them, but non-matching wood shows less in the C if a different rib has to be used and the lower and the upper ribs will still match. Plane straight the edge of the rib that will be glued to the back, indicated by arrows, following the grain lines as closely as possible. Then plane the top edge, leaving all ribs 1mm higher than the block to which they will be glued – sometimes they shrink across the grain when heated. The ends of the ribs should be square to the planed edge which will be glued to the back. Ribs should be left somewhere slightly damp, such as on a concrete floor for a day before they are bent. To be damp right through is better than to apply water to the surface since this may cause ribs to distort.

CRAMPING BLOCKS

Cramping blocks may be made from lime or some similar, easy to work wood. The top, bottom and corner blocks should follow the template. The upper two corner blocks and the lower two can be made as one double-height block and then sawn in half; the steps for cramping the C-curves must be at right angles to the base. The backs of the blocks should be parallel to the sides of the hole in the mould.

A mould with all the rib-cramping blocks in place.

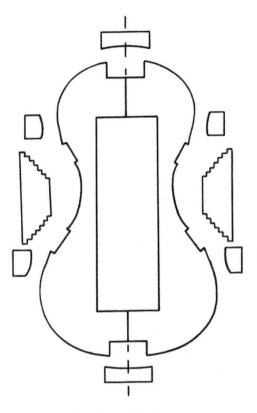

THE BENDING IRON

The bending iron should have a slightly smaller radius than the curve to be bent. A 60mm-diameter tube squashed into an ellipse, one end having a 10mm radius and the other one of 15mm is suitable for violins and violas; cellos need a tube with a diameter of 120mm squashed to larger curves. The heating mechanism must be capable of maintaining a steady temperature of about 150°C. If you take a piece of paper and hold it against the bending iron it must not scorch. Be aware that the numbers on commercial bending irons have no exact meaning and cannot be compared one with another. A cooker element embedded in sand will do or a heating coil specially made for the purpose, with a thermoregulator. As ribs used to be bent on a solid bar of metal that had been heated in a fire, this must be a

possibility too. Also make a bending strap about 150mm long from 0.2mm metal or stiff leather, with handles or blocks of wood to grip.

It is wise to keep a pot of water handy, not for wetting the ribs but for testing the heat of the iron: a drop of water should just bounce off the iron. (If your finger touches the iron you can quickly dunk your finger in it.) Having prepared the ribs, cramping blocks and bending iron, it is time to shape the inside curve of the corner blocks for the C-rib.

C-CURVE SHAPING

Place the template on the top of the blocks, align it with a square and carefully draw round it. Extend the C-curve line 3mm beyond the points and split off any superfluous wood.

It is possible to gouge against the bench, as in the photograph, or downwards on to a board, but by whichever method, try to produce a flowing curve. As the purfling follows the rib line, it is good to think of the purfling corners. The two curves must meet and stop where they join. If the curves are too flat they collide, if they are too deep they meet but want to open out again and are also more difficult to bend. The shape of the C-curve is critical to the beauty of the outline so it is worth spending time on it. Keep the gouged surface of the blocks square to the base so that the back and the front will have similar outlines.

BENDING

To bend the middle of a straight piece of rib usually leads to a point forming which becomes a crack, so when bending the C-ribs try to begin the curve immediately at the very beginning. This piece of rib will eventually be cut off, so that if it cracks it is unimportant; if it curves well, the next piece of rib that will be part of the violin will bend to a better curve.

Locating the template on the blocks and drawing around it.

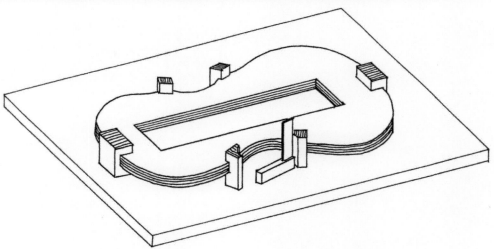

Using a square to check that the blocks are upright.

Begin with the upper tighter curve. Hold the end of the rib firmly against the iron with a block of wood, trying to keep the free hand relaxed as it gently pulls the rib round. Once the curve is begun use the bending strap and pull the rib close to the iron, continuing the curve by moving the rib steadily beyond the end of the iron until it will extend at least 3mm past the edge of the corner block. If it takes longer than 5 minutes to bend the curve the wood will dry out and be more likely to crack. Having succeeded with the upper curve, begin at the other end

One method of gouging a C-curve.

little more to achieve an exact fit. Then find steps in the cramping blocks that slightly push the ends of the rib apart, with the back of the cramping block as parallel to the side of the hole in the mould as possible.

Cramp lightly in place and check underneath. When both ribs are fitted and cramped, mark the steps on the cramping blocks to be used and make a pencil mark across the rib and corner block. Remove the cramping block, holding the rib down while doing so, and then remove the rib. Rub dry soap on the edge of the mould, put glue on the corner blocks and cramp the rib exactly in the same place. Occasionally there are ribs that will not bend and in these cases wet a double strip of thin cloth, such as a bit of old sheet, and place between the rib and the bending iron, and proceed as before.

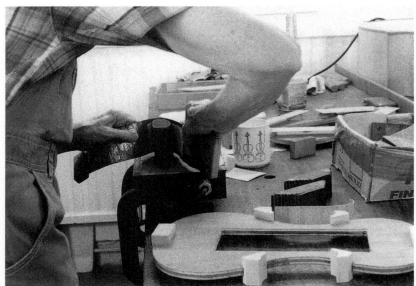

Bending the end of a C-rib.

of the rib, using the wider end of the bending iron and bend until the rib fits the lower corner block. It may now be necessary to bend the middle of the rib a

Cramping a C rib gently in place.

SHAPING BLOCKS FOR UPPER AND LOWER RIBS

When the glue has dried (at least 2 hours later) remove the cramping blocks. Extend the line that was drawn round the template on the corner blocks across the top edge of the C-rib. Trim the ends of these ribs exactly square to base, just beyond the end of this new line.

Always start cutting at each edge of the rib and cut towards the centre of the rib height; if you cut past an edge the wood may split along the grain.

Fitting all curves to their respective cramping blocks and keeping them square to base, shape the end blocks and then the corner blocks. The feather edge at the ends of the ribs is very delicate and should be shaped last.

Bend the upper and lower ribs, leaving extra rib extending beyond the C-rib.

Trim the other end of the ribs to length if necessary, checking that they are square

and making a perfect butt joint on the bottom block.

Glue and cramp the ribs to the bottom block, and then, holding the rib snugly

Bending the corner curve of a longer rib.

Checking the fit of the lower ribs where they meet.

Cramping a lower rib at a corner block, with an extra pair of hands.

against the mould, glue and cramp the corner blocks, checking the rib for squareness. Another pair of hands to do up the cramps is very useful.

Repeat this for the upper ribs, although here the joint is not so critical since it will be cut away. When the glue is dry, trim back the ends of these four ribs to within 0.5mm of the C-ribs.

FLATTENING

Put a chamfer across the inside edge of the corner blocks and the corners of the end blocks to within 2mm of the ribs.

Flatten both edges of the ribs and blocks, testing on a flat surface until they are perfectly flat and with the ribs at the correct height.

The advantage of planing, holding the ribs against the bench, is that it is possible to see what the plane is doing. It is also possible to flatten ribs if they are sitting on the bench or a flat surface and with cellos it is the only possible way. Check with a straight edge that the block ends are not angled in any way, and particularly that the tips of the corners are not rounded down.

LININGS

The linings may be made from a similar wood to the blocks and a strip of wood can be planed, as the ribs were, to the correct thickness. One edge is then planed smooth and a strip cut off by using a cutting gauge and knife.

The edge is then planed smooth again before the next strip is cut. As the linings are thicker than the ribs, they will change the rib outline unless they are bent to the exact shape of the rib. The wood from which the linings are made may also move differently to the ribs and it is wise to leave a 0.5mm gap for expansion on each side of the end blocks. At the corner blocks the linings are let in, either in a tapered V-shape or square-ended, at each end of the C-curve.

It is not necessary to let them in on the lower and upper curves as they are held in place by the curve. Having bent and fitted the linings with the smooth edge down, glue them in by using clothes pegs, positioning the linings slightly proud of the rib edge and checking that no glue spreads

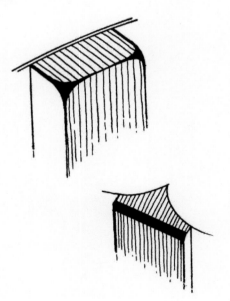

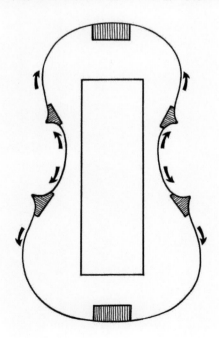

LEFT: *Areas of the blocks which should be bevelled.*

Directions in which the ribs should be planed.

Using a knife to bevel the blocks

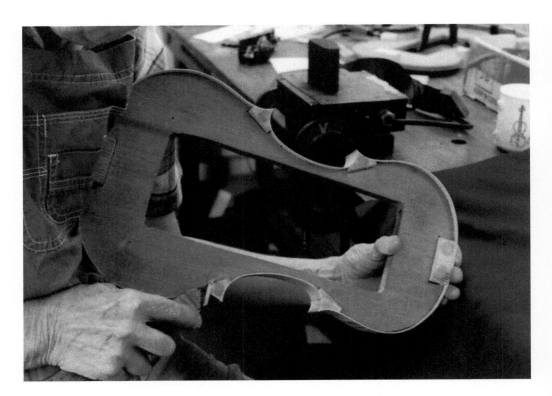

Planing the edges of the ribs.

Cutting the strips for linings.

ABOVE: The linings are let into the blocks (not wedged between block and rib).

Sawing the first side of the V for the lining.

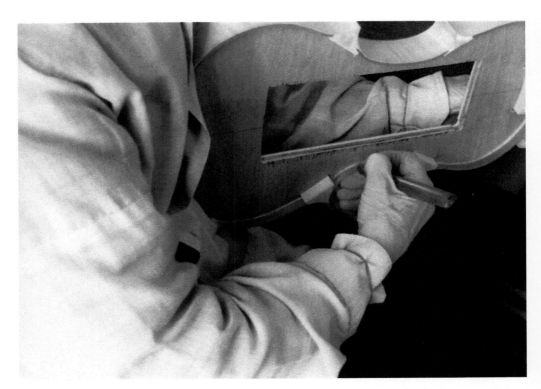

ABOVE: The shape in section to which the lining is bevelled.

Bevelling the lining with a small knife.

down towards the mould. Glue the linings only to the edge of the ribs that will be glued to the back. When gluing the linings to the C-curves, peg from the centre outwards. When gluing the linings to the upper and lower ribs, begin pegging the lining close to the corner block. This will ensure that the gap occurs close to the top and bottom block. The other linings may be left in place or fitted later. Reflatten the edge of the ribs with the linings glued in.

These linings are now bevelled back on the inside edge to as near nothing as possible, without scratching the rib, thus getting rid of a discontinuity and a line which would be prone to crack if the rib were knocked. A short-bladed knife is best for this, and it can be held like a pencil with the second finger running along the top of the rib and the lining, controlling the depth of the cut. The linings may then be sandpapered smooth.

5 BEGINNING THE BACK AND THE FRONT

Planing a centre join by pushing the wood over the plane.

Having completed the ribs it is time to move on to the big pieces of wood, though eventually you will be left with less than 20 per cent of the pieces with which you begin. It is well to bear this in mind when making the joints in the back and the front. If the two halves do not bond as one piece of wood the shell, which will become the back or front of the instrument and which will be less than 3mm thick in places, will have weaknesses along the joint. As with so many things, errors made early on may grow into bigger problems.

JOINTS

Before joining the halves of the back and the front try to ascertain how the wood will split. Plane the faces that will begin as the flat sides of the plates, following the split line unless this leaves too little height for the arching. The joint may be planed in three ways:

- by using a shooting board;
- by holding the wedge in a vice, being careful not to stress it, and pushing the

Wedges incompletely sawn, and after being joined.

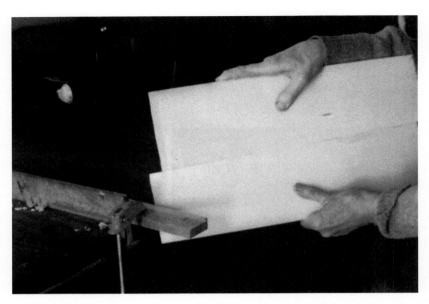

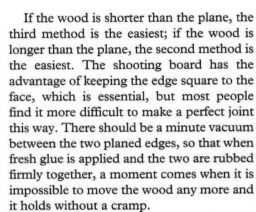

If the wood is shorter than the plane, the third method is the easiest; if the wood is longer than the plane, the second method is the easiest. The shooting board has the advantage of keeping the edge square to the face, which is essential, but most people find it more difficult to make a perfect joint this way. There should be a minute vacuum between the two planed edges, so that when fresh glue is applied and the two are rubbed firmly together, a moment comes when it is impossible to move the wood any more and it holds without a cramp.

If possible, the two faces should line up. The alignment may be improved by tapping one half or the other against the edge of the bench.

Some 4 hours later, when the glue is really dry, it should be possible to put the back plate on the floor, wedge side down, and stand on it. (But be cautious if you weigh more than 16 stones.) Do not try this with the front, as the wood might split.

Rubbing the centre join.

LEFT: *Adjusting the alignment of a cello joint with a mallet.*

RIGHT: *Planing the flat surface of the back, holding it in a jig.*

plane along the edge of the wedge; or
● by holding the plane in a vice and pushing the wood over the plane.

FLATTENING THE PLATES

When the glue is dry, test the flat side on a flat surface and plane off any high spots that show up. It is possible to hold the plate in a Workmate; but if you have nothing suitable, make a jig, as in the photograph, lining the holding blocks with sandpaper for a better grip.

The cramps support half the wedge and the other side may be supported with a matching wedge. After planing, the final test is to put the ribs on the back and then on the front and ensure that there are no little gaps anywhere. If there are, the glue would probably hold, but the plate would be stressed by being forced into a hole and the back or the front would not be free to vibrate fully. When everything fits, mark all centre lines exactly with a sharp, soft pencil. To find the centre line on the top block of the ribs, measure the full upper bout width, mark on the plate half this width on each side of the centre line. With the centre lines lined up at the bottom, place your upper ribs between these two marks. Mark on the ribs the centre from the plate. A line can then be drawn here square to the flat side of the ribs. Draw the exact outline and a sawing line 4–5mm away from the rib by putting the pencil in a washer that runs round against the rib.

DETERMINING THE SHAPE OF THE CORNERS

On the flat side draw a line diagonally from the end of a top rib corner to the opposite lower corner. Measure, from where this line crosses the centre line, the distance to the top of the rib line and mark the same distance down towards the bottom block.

Draw a line at the end of the washer line at the lower corners, lined up to the top rib line, and, at the end of the washer line, at the upper corners to the lower mark. In this way the ends of all the top corners will

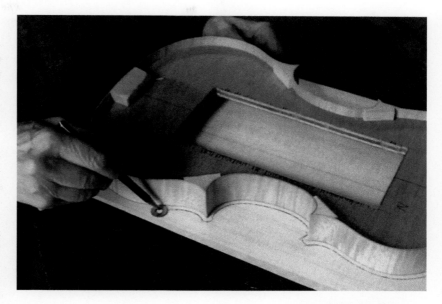

ABOVE: *Drawing the outline of the back, using a washer.*

How to determine the angles to which the ends of the corners should be drawn.

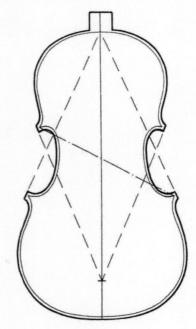

line up and similarly the lower corners. Continue the sawing line to this new line in a curve that is slightly further from the rib line on the outside curves. Mark out the button on the back at least 5mm wider and higher than the finished measurements.

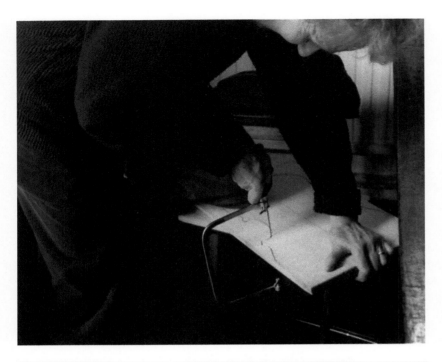

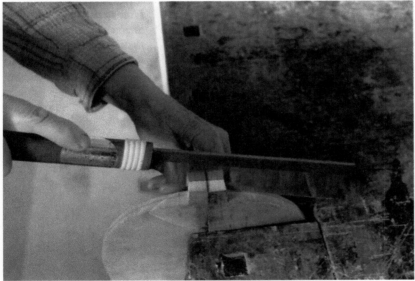

TOP: *Sawing out the back without stressing the centre join.*

ABOVE: *Sawing the button and top edge to thickness.*

SAWING OUT

It is important not to put too much stress on the centre joint; but instead of holding the plate down with a knee on a stool, it may also be cramped down, but saw on the side that is cramped.

Those with access to a bandsaw will prefer to use it. If the flat side of the wedge rests on the sawtable, the sawn edge will be only slightly out of square on the generous side. The more smoothly and accurately you saw, the easier the trimming of the edges will be.

ROUGH-ARCHING

Using a marking gauge, mark on the sawn edge the finished edge thickness plus 0.5mm and the arching height plus 1mm. Plane down the top of the plates to the upper lines. On the outside of the front measure down from the top edge the length of the bodystop and mark half the length of the f-hole on each side of this point on the centre line. This last line forms the top of the cylindrical shape that lies between the f-holes. For the present, draw a rectangle 5mm all around this line. On the back, find the same point on the outside that you found on the inside by drawing lines diagonally from corner to corner and draw an ellipse that extends about 5mm on each side of this point and 20mm up and down. The back also has a cylindrical feel to its arching, but since, when it is hollowed out, it will be thicker in the centre and the inside should be gently concave, the outside of the back is a continuous curve from end to end. For the moment, it is close to a catenary curve – the curve formed by letting a chain fixed at both ends hang down. Make a pushing board, a piece of plywood with a batten fixed on the underside that will hook over the edge of the bench, and two curves fixed to the upper side against which the plates can be pushed. Alternatively, let two 25mm dowels, with slots cut into them, into the bench to hold the plates in place. The aim now is to form a narrow platform 10mm in from the lower and upper curves, across the corners and 6mm in from the C-curves down to the thickness of the edge line, and a gentle curve from this platform up to the areas marked around the centre lines. It is safer to saw the button to thickness, so cut down outside the marking gauge line round the edges of the button into the edge of the back curve. Then saw across the back, being careful not to saw into the thickness of the edge, to remove this piece of wood.

Gouge either with or across the grain; both have their disadvantages. If the plate is gouged across the grain the scooping action of the tool may make the arching too flat or almost hollow where it should be rounded, particularly in the C-curve where the arching rises steeply. However, this direction of gouging is good on highly figured maple which, if gouged with the grain, may split down into the waves.

The danger of gouging the other way, with the grain, is removing too much wood where the gouging directions meet in the C-curve. If enough wood is first removed across the corners – which are flat at this stage – this is less likely to happen.

It is important to develop a feel for how wood splits along the grain. Imagine the plate as layers built up from the flat side. If the wood had been well cut and planed correctly, the layers will be parallel to the flat side; if not, each side will split down towards an opposite end. Spruce, in particular, splits easily with the grain, so never gouge against its grain.

Trim the edge thickness line with a knife and then gouge the edge platform as exactly as possible.

EDGE THICKNESSING

Having rough-arched the back and the front, the edges must now be made to the exact thickness. It is difficult to make a surface parallel to the flat side of the plate on the edge of a slope, so cut a small channel with the 10mm-gouge, 6mm in from the outline. Using a flat chisel and file and checking the thickness with a vernier calliper, smooth all the edges and complete

ABOVE: *Gouging across the back.*

Directions in which it should be possible to gouge.

the edge platform. If there is now a step up to the arching, gouge it away before smoothing out the arching curve with the 36mm-plane. If the maple will not plane smoothly, try holding the plane at an angle to the direction of the plane stroke; in other words, hold the plane crookedly.

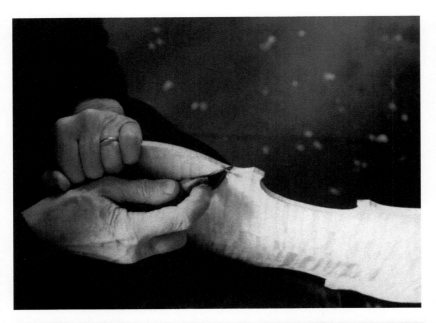

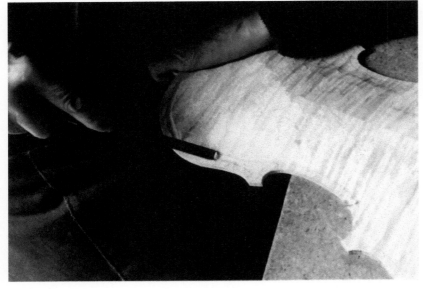

TOP: Bevelling the edge to thickness.

ABOVE: Gouging a channel before flattening the edge.

OUTLINE

The outline is easier to trim if the back and the front are temporarily glued to the ribs with spots of glue on all the blocks, keeping the glue away from the ribs and lining up the centre lines carefully. If the flat sides of the plates have not moved this is relatively simple, especially if four cramping blocks that are slightly wedge-shaped and covered with leather have been prepared for cramping the end blocks. However, the plates may warp. As they are thick in the middle and thin round the edges, these may curve up at the sides, and the joint may even come open at the ends. If this happens, put the plate, usually the back, on a concrete floor and the joint should go back together and more glue can be rubbed into the joint. It should then dry before being cramped to the ribs.

The tools needed for trimming the edges are the 18mm-knife, the 36mm-plane and the vernier calliper. The general overhang is 2.5–3mm but it is wider at the corners.

Find a good picture to copy. As a general guide, the top corners are 7mm with 3mm on the inside curve and the outside curve widening gradually from the basic overhang to 4mm. The lower corners are 8mm, divided in the same proportions.

The Xs on the diagram indicate places where the directions of the grain meet and extra care must be taken there not to make the curve too deep. The outside curves are particularly shallow.

When all the curves are satisfactory, file lightly across both edges at once to ensure that they are parallel to the ribs. Too much filing causes bumps in the edge of the spruce since the file is a lazy tool and removes more soft wood than hard grain lines. It is more effective on end grain.

If the edges are not truly square, the leg of the purfling marker will waver and the purfling will not run parallel to the outline.

PREPARING FOR PURFLING

Nowadays purfling can be bought made with a 0.7mm maple centre and fibre or blackened wood outsides 0.3mm thick. Guitar-makers use more widely varying inlays which are also suitable for the violin family or purfling can be made and even preformed into suitable curves. Whatever your choice, set the blades of the purfling

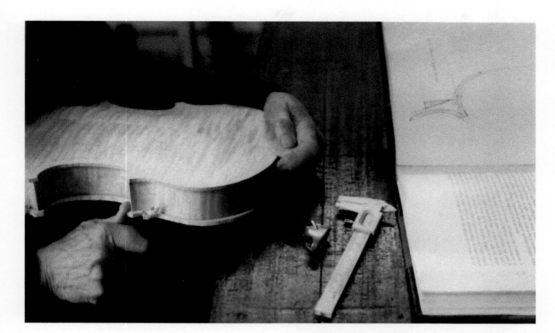

Trimming the outline, with the back and the front temporarily glued to the ribs.

BELOW LEFT: Directions in which the edge must be cut.

BELOW RIGHT: Squaring the edges with a file.

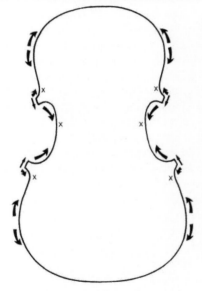

marker to the correct width, with the outside blade about 4mm in from the edge. If the corners are small this distance should be less and, conversely, more for wide corners and, of course, cellos. Try marking a purfling groove across the grain of a spruce off-cut – cut the groove deeper with a craft knife, the tip rubbed in soap, and clean the groove out with a pick of exactly the same width as the purfling. The purfling should be an easy fit in this groove since the wood will swell when the glue is applied, and tight purfling builds in unwanted stresses.

If the groove is good sit the body in its cradle and mark firmly, but not deeply, round all the edges except for the last 5mm at the ends of the C-curves and the

Using a purfling marker, with the body sitting in a cradle.

RIGHT: Picking out the purfling groove.

BELOW: Marking the purfling line at a corner, using a gouge.

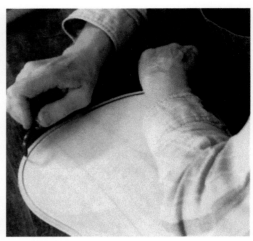

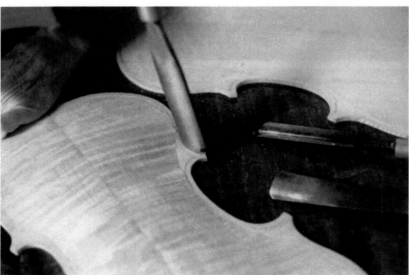

into the end of the purfling marker line and let it continue to your chosen point. On the outside curve do the same, using a gouge with a flatter curve.

The inside curve must flow up into the outside lines. To mark the line where the purfling passes below the button, make a template in thin wood, copying the curve following the top edge of the front plate. Cut along it, joining the lines left by the purfling marker. When cutting the groove to depth it is important not to cut too deeply at this point because the button has to withstand the pull of the neck and the back must not be weakened.

Using the craft knife, cut the groove to a depth of half the thickness of the edge. The later stages of the back groove can be made easier to cut by rubbing dry soap into the groove to reduce friction on the sides of the blade. When cutting the lines deeper be particularly careful not to take any short cuts across the curves. It is important to cut deep enough. If the groove is not deep enough, there will be no purfling left when the purfling channel is gouged. Ensure that the bottom of the groove is smooth – a hole is slightly better than a bump, as the purfling will pass over a hole but be held up by a bump. A clean purfling groove makes the next stage of inlaying the purfling much easier.

last 20mm on the outside curve. Take the thin, old, table knife, insert it cautiously between the ribs and the plates and pop the back and the front off the ribs, protecting your holding hand. To complete the marking out, refer back to the shaping of the rib curves, then choose the point where you want the purfling to meet. Either draw or mark, using the curves of the 30mm- and the 20mm-gouge for the curves at the corners. The lines nearest the edge should be marked first, beginning with the C-curve. Put the gouge

6 THE BACK AND THE FRONT CONTINUED

PURFLING

Elegant corners will not make an instrument sound better, but they are a sign of competent craftsmanship and a pleasure to look at. If the groove has been well cut they are also possible. First ensure that the tips of the corners of the grooves at the ends of the Cs curve towards each other and that there is no straight line. If straight strips of purfling are being used it is worth bending them, especially at the ends.

There are two common ways of fitting the purfling: either fit all the purfling dry and put pencil marks across it and the plate to ensure that the purfling strips are put back exactly in the right place and then glue, as described below, or glue in the C-curves first as follows. If the purfling strips in the C-curves are glued in first they should have barely angled ends.

TOP: *The purfling at a C-curve before being trimmed.*
ABOVE: *A corner with black meeting black on both sides of the white.*

These ends are trimmed further from the inside corner to the outside point of the corner, much as the end of the C-rib was trimmed to a feather edge.

Continue the cut at the outside point if you want to extend the outside black to a

TOP: *Bending the purfling for the C-curve.*

ABOVE: *Trimming the end of the purfling at a C-curve.*

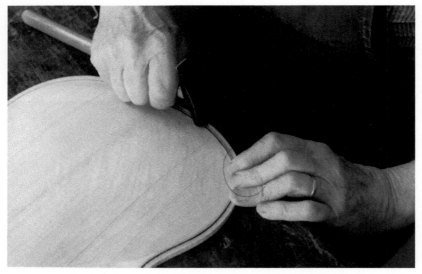

purfling around the top and the lower bout or use two pieces joined with a scarf joint in the thickness of the purfling.

On the front, glue in only one C-curve purfling at a time so that it is still malleable when the next pieces are glued in. A little gap may be left at the centre joints since the purfling will be removed later when the neck and the saddle are fitted. The glue should be thinner than usual and the purfling should be quickly pushed into place with fingers, gently tapped with a little hammer, if necessary, and then pushed right down to the bottom of the groove again with the hammer until all the surplus glue has been squeezed out.

The groove should be warmed before the glue is applied so that it stays liquid longer and will squeeze out better. After the purfling has been pushed down, all visible glue should be wiped off with a warm, wet rag.

GOUGING THE PURFLING

Draw a line halfway between the edge and the purfling, except at the corners, where the distance from the purfling remains constant. When the glue is dry, gouge down at least 1mm with the 10mm gouge, staying on the purfling side of this line.

The edges of the instrument must be thick enough to withstand wear; but in from the edge, where the internal hollowing out of the plate will begin, the front should be more than 1mm thinner than the edge thickness. If, later on, this should entail the need to gouge down steeply on the inside, this sudden curve will stiffen the plate. Therefore it is better to gouge the purfling bravely and then, with a larger, flatter gouge, sweep up from the purfling into the arching curve.

TOP LEFT: Fitting the second piece of purfling at a corner.

TOP RIGHT: A scarf joint in the purfling.

ABOVE: Pressing the purfling into the groove with a hammer.

longer point. There are two possibilities. The cut can be straight, so that, if the line were continued to the corner, two-thirds of the corner should be above it and one-third below. Or the two cuts at the ends of the corners should curve slightly towards each other. For either method it is easier to use the point of the craft knife held upside down as a fine purfling pick.

Now fit the purfling strip in the outside curves. Either use only one piece of

Different makers scoop by different amounts. Gouging too deep may lead to problems and particularly on the front, for if you cut below the split of the wood, it is difficult to scrape across the area on each side of the centre join. (Whatever you do, do not gouge away the 'cylinder' between the f-holes.)

FINISHING THE ARCHING

Smooth round the purfling with the smaller thumb plane, then smooth the general arching with the larger thumb plane, using a small straight edge to look for bumps.

On the back look for a continuous curve swooping down to the purfling. On the front let the arching spring a little more quickly from the purfling and keep the central cylinder. Draw contour lines with the pencil calliper, then plane more until the contour lines are parallel to the outline round the lower and the upper curve and as straight as possible in the centre.

Be careful with arching templates (if you use them) and calliper lines that you use them only as a general guide and not as predetermined curves. With these aids it is easy to lose the flow of the arching. Draw the f-holes on the front and, looking at the arching from the side, check that the surface the f-hole lies on is reasonably straight and that enough wood has been removed across the corners. Do not worry if the lower end of the f-hole looks as though it is a little higher than the top end for this is almost inevitable.

SCRAPING

Flexible, small scrapers are best for finishing the arching because stiff ones make flats instead of a continuous curve. Little scrapers may be sharpened with a square edge like a cabinet scraper and then burred over with a steel or the smooth back of a small, round chisel or

ABOVE: *Gouging round the purfling groove.*

LEFT: *The purfling should be gouged down by at least 1mm.*

they may be sharpened at an angle like a chisel edge all the way round and then lightly burred or left just as a sharp edge which leaves a good finish. Mainly use a

Gouging the scoop of the arching, up from the purfling.

scraper about 60mm by 40mm, with two more rounded and two less rounded corners for scraping round the purfling. Low sunlight shows up humps and hollows well, but, failing that, hold the plate on edge under a lamp when the shadow will highlight the faults. As yet do not scrape the area from the edge of the f-hole down to the purfling, but when the rest is scraped draw on the f-holes exactly.

PLACING F-HOLES

On violas and small instruments that have no fixed body-stop draw a line joining the lower purfling curve of the bottom corners. Place the f-hole template so that this line passes across the top of the lower hole and mark where the inside f-hole nick will come. Draw a line at right angles to the centre join at this point. This now defines the body stop and from this the neck stop may later be calculated. On full-size violins and cellos the body stop is usually standard. With pencil compasses set to the distance from the outside edge of the front to the lower hole, draw a line parallel to the outline and then mark the

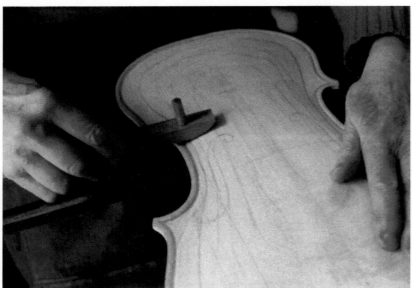

TOP: *Planing the arching smooth.*

ABOVE: *Checking the arching curves for symmetry, and in relation to the f-hole.*

RIGHT: *The shape of contour lines on the back.*

CENTRE: *The shape of contour lines on the front.*

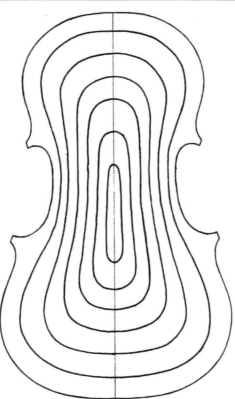

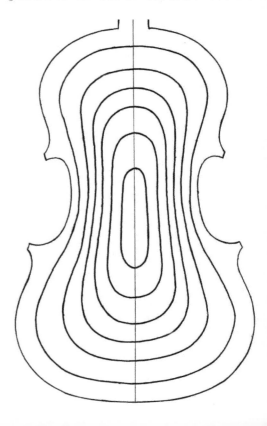

distance between the top holes of the f-holes. Using these three points, locate the f-hole template and draw the f-holes with a soft, sharp pencil. With gouge, plane and scraper gently hollow the lower wing of the f-hole and blend the hollowing into the arching slope at the top corner.

HOLLOWING OUT

Before gouging at all, mark on the flat side of the plates the areas to which the ribs, linings and blocks will glue. These surfaces must never be removed.

Set the pencil calliper to 2mm more than the greatest thickness of the plate being gouged and draw a line on the flat side. This line comes where the plate is the thickness to which the calliper was set and all the area inside it is thicker. Fix the plate gently in the cradle with turn buttons or use the slots in the bench nails. When the plate and the cradle are firmly held, gouge across, removing the calliper line, unless it crosses the gluing areas, and take shavings right across past the centre join.

When this has been done from both sides, draw a new calliper line and repeat the process until the calliper leaves no mark. On the back, reset the calliper 2mm smaller and gouge the top and the lower

area thinner while leaving the centre untouched. Using the pencil calliper more exactly, plane the plates to within 0.5mm of the thickness given in the tables.

If copying an old instrument, it is unwise to follow its thicknesses exactly every piece of wood is different.

Set the point calliper to 1mm over the exact thicknesses and prick the areas to be worked on. Plane only just sufficiently to remove the prick marks. *See* photos on page 51.

If the plate is now suspended between finger and thumb, holding a point 60mm in from the top curve, and then tapped with a finger between the f-holes on the centre line (or a similar place on the back), it should be possible to hear a clear tone. If the pitch is as given, only scrape the surface smooth gently; if it is higher, set the point calliper narrower and plane more and then scrape.

Thinning the area between the C-curves lowers the pitch most; but take care that the edges just inside the gluing areas around the outer curves are not too thick, although do not scoop down too quickly inside the gluing areas left for the top and bottom blocks. It is unwise to thin below 2.5mm on violins, 4mm on 'cello fronts and 3.5mm on cello backs. Sometimes with very strong wood it is not possible to

---

Thicknessing and Tuning the Plates

Make the front of uniform thickness except for the region around the f-holes: violin and viola, 3mm (ffs 3.2mm) and cello 4.5mm (ffs 5mm). Suspend between the finger and thumb and tap for the pitch of the plate; then thin it uniformly until sounding f (violin); C (viola); and CC (cello).

The back should be graded smoothly from the thickest point (A) outwards, obtaining the thicknesses shown in the table; the main upper and lower areas (E and F) should be uniform.

	A	B	C	D	E	F
Violin and viola	5	4.5	4	3.5	2.6	2.8
Cello	8	7	6	5	3.5	4

Then thin uniformly to sound: f# (violin); C# (viola); and CC# (cello), if possible. Measurements made with a pencil calliper will be generous; those made with the point calliper will be mean.

Fluting the wing of the f-hole (preferably before the front is hollowed out).

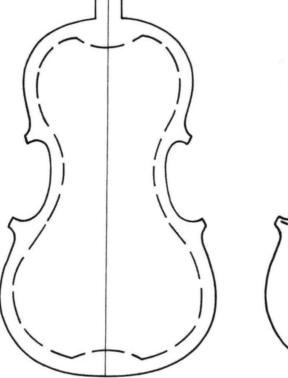

LEFT: Marking the areas to which the blocks, ribs and linings will be glued, before gouging.

RIGHT: Plan for thicknessing the back.

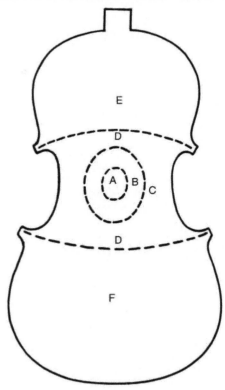

Gouging out the back.

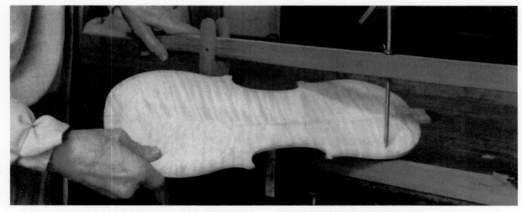

Using the point caliper to mark the thickness.

Scraping the inside of the back smooth.

get down to the suggested pitches; however, a tap tone that rings well is more important than the exact pitch.

It is also possible to check the thickness of the front by holding it up to a light source. Dark patches will be thicker unless they follow the grain lines and the dark strip will probably indicate denser wood. These areas could be made thinner, but a corrugated inside to the plate would lead to problems in fitting the bass-bar and the soundpost and it is better to aim for the smoothest finish possible.

STUDS

Once the thickness of the back is finished, it is better to put studs on the centre join if you have any doubts about its strength or if the grain wiggles about its join. This is especially true if you are planning to put the instrument in a drying cabinet after varnishing it. Take a strip of unfigured maple about 10mm wide and plane one side flat. Plane the other side to a thickness of 1.5mm and then round these sides down from the centre of the width. With dividers mark out 10mm lengths and cut down to the marks from both sides on a slope, so that the squares of wood are bevelled on opposite sides. They are already rounded down on the other two sides. With the flat side down, glue seven of these, equidistantly spaced, across the join with the grain of the stud at right angles to the back; just press them down, there is no need to cramp them. When the glue is dry, smooth them with sandpaper.

F-HOLES

Cramp a piece of wood with a V-slot in it to the bench. Improve the pencil drawing of the f-hole and then take the square-bladed bradawl and, rotating more than pushing against a supporting finger, make a hole by the outside f-nick and thread through a fine fretsaw blade and tension it in the saw.

Saw down just inside the pencil line, turn and cut along the straight line, then round the hole, anti-clockwise on the bass f-hole and clockwise on the treble. Then saw back up towards the top and repeat these directions round the top hole, then saw down to where you started from. Trim the holes with a very sharp knife, carefully holding the front flat on the bench and cutting from underneath. Follow the arrows on the diagram – always cutting with the grain.

The corner of the hole is less likely to break off if it is well supported, so cut it exactly before continuing round the hole, then take care not to cut too far where the arrows meet. Slightly undercut the holes; some makers even undercut along the shaft too. The shaft must be sufficiently wide so that a soundpost of the correct thickness easily passes through it. You can also use a file to smooth the curves, but it is difficult to do this without removing the crispness of the knife cuts. To make the nicks, cut in at right angles to the shaft, angle in from both sides to this cut then make even smaller cuts to make the second and the third cut flow in from the edge of the f-hole.

BASS-BAR

On the inside of the front draw a line joining the inner nicks.

From this line measure up to the top edge of the front and mark one-quarter of this distance down from the top edge; then measure down to the bottom edge and measure one-quarter of this distance up from there. These marks give the length of the bass-bar. Since the bass-bar should be placed 1mm in from the outside edge of the foot of the bridge, measure the total width of the bridge feet. Mark half this width from the centre join of the front at the lower end where the mark for the length of the bar comes and mark half this width minus 2mm at the top end. These marks give the position of the side of the

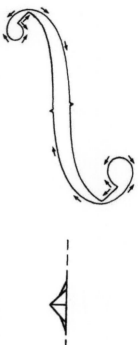

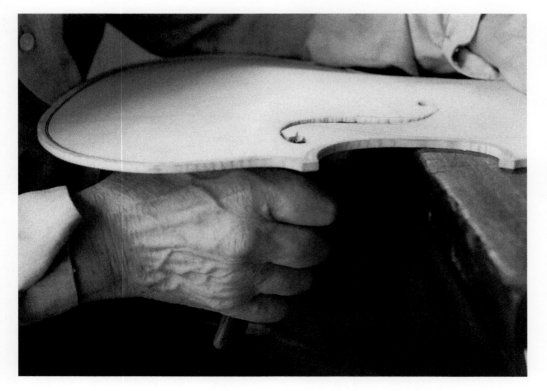

FAR LEFT: *Using a sawing V while fretsawing the f-hole.*

TOP: *The directions in which f-holes must be cut.*

LEFT: *Cutting an f-hole.*

ABOVE: *Making the f-hole nicks with five cuts.*

Positioning the bass-bar.

BELOW: *Using a knife to fit the bass-bar.*

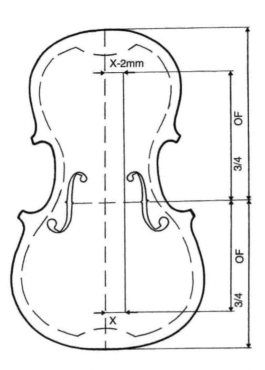

bass-bar furthest from the centre line. Remember that this should be done on the bass side of the instrument. Plane one side of the bass-bar flat, following both the side grain and the end grain, then plane the other side to the correct thickness. Split a piece off one long edge. Removing equal amounts of wood from both ends of this split edge, gradually make it fit the curve of the front. The bar should be slightly more curved than the front to help it eventually support the pressure of the strings on the bridge. If the bar is cramped only on the f-nick line there should be a gap gradually increasing from this cramp position to 0.5mm (1mm for cellos) at the ends. If the bar is cramped at the ends it should fit perfectly without twisting the front and be at right-angles to the end-block gluing areas. The fitting may be done with a knife or a chisel, and soft, white chalk may be rubbed on the front so

Gluing in the bass-bar.

that, if the bar is moved fractionally back and forth, it will pick up chalk on the high spots. Check the following points:

- The bar should rock evenly about the f-nick line.
- As you rock the bar from end to end, it must not twist but remain perpendicular to the plane of the gluing areas.
- The surface of the bar must not be rounded across its width.
- When the bar is held close against the front, the bar must fit well, but particularly at the ends.

When the bar fits perfectly, brush off all the chalk and put a spot of glue on the front where the ends come and glue all along the bar.

Cramp the ends first and be careful not to push the bar sideways with the centre cramp and the intermediate ones. Do not force the cramps on too firmly. When the glue is dry sit the front in a cradle and take the bar down to the correct heights at the centre and the ends. (The 'wrong' end of the vernier calliper is useful to check the height.) The outline should be straight for the length of the f-holes, sweeping down to the ends.

In cross-section it should be semi-circular at the ends and elliptical in the middle, with the shaping coming down as near as possible to the front.

The smallest plane works well and the sides may then be filed smooth, keeping a finger over the end of the file so it does not scratch the front. The bar may then be sandpapered smooth. Finally bevel down the ends of the bar from 8mm in from the ends, down to nothing at the ends. It is difficult to decide exactly how much wood to take off the bass-bar, but if you have made a note of the pitch of the front after it was thicknessed, it should now be the same. When the f-holes are cut, the pitch of the front goes down by a minor third. After the bass bar is fitted it will be higher than the original pitch, and when the bass-bar is shaped it should be back where it started.

Shaping the profile of the bass-bar with knife and plane.

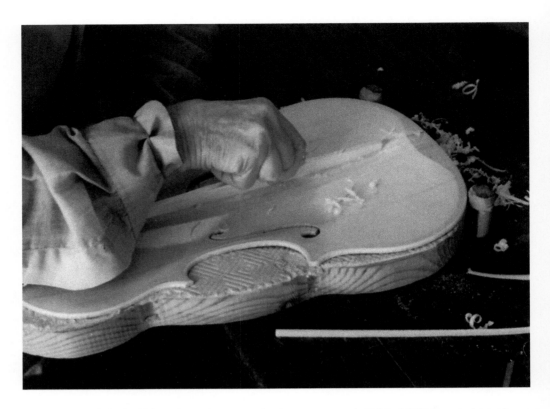

Rounding the sides of the bass-bar with the small plane.

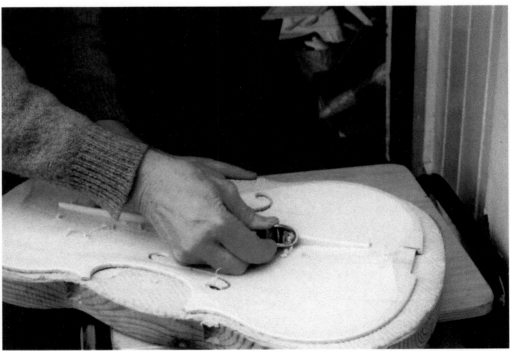

7 ASSEMBLING THE BODY

GLUING ON THE BACK

The edges of the back and the front will eventually be rounded and it is easier to shape the under edge before gluing the back to the ribs.

To get an even rounding, it helps to put a little bevel on the edge just outside the rib line. Use a crossing file on the inside curves and a flat file on the outside curves, working along the edge, rounding it to almost half the thickness of the edge. The rounding

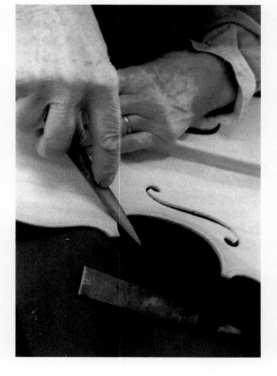

may then be scraped smooth or sand-papered, taking care not to remove the rib line yet. After the under edge is finished, the flat area of the back, to which the ribs, linings and blocks will be glued, must be cleaned and the rib line will then go. However, leave a mark where the rib line crosses the centre join under the button which will help to locate the ribs in the correct place. The centre joint at the lower end should be marked on the curved edge. The ribs too should be scraped or papered clean; if using sandpaper on these surfaces, wrap it tightly around a piece of wood or even glue it on, so that the edges of the ribs are not rounded. Again leave the centre line marked on the top rib and at the lower rib if there is no join. On cellos particularly it is wise to drill the endpin hole before the mould is taken out. Mark the centre of the rib height on the centre line and make a lead hole, then drill a hole, smaller than the reamer to be used, straight through the end block. Both sides of the ribs should also be retested for flatness because the temporary gluing may make the end grain of the blocks swell and once the mould has been removed it is difficult to plane the blocks and the edges of the ribs.

At last the time has come to trim back the ends of the upper and the lower ribs to the feather edge of the C ribs, making sure that the ends are square and cutting with the block plane from the edges to the middle of the rib height. The feather edge should not show at all. Using two slightly wedged blocks covered in leather, cramp the ribs to the back at the end blocks, then, pressing the edges gently, check that the fit is perfect. If not, mark the doubtful places with an arrow on the ribs, which can later

TOP: The inside edges of the back and front have to be rounded.

BOTTOM: Using a file to round the inside edge.

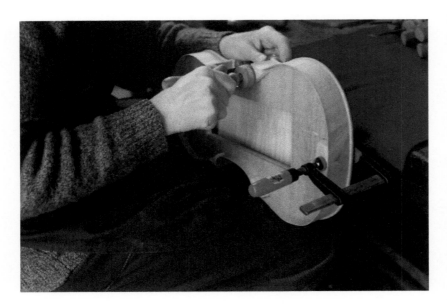

TOP: *Gluing the back to the ribs.*

BOTTOM: *Sawing the sides of the saddle recess.*

but there should not be much glue showing.

Remember that soft glue is easy to remove but hard glue is difficult.

If later the ribs separate from the back a little more glue may be inserted with a clean, thin table knife, the edges recramped and again any visible glue cleaned off.

THE SADDLE

The saddle is cut from a piece of very hard wood such as ebony – an old piano key will make both the nut and the saddle. As it is difficult to see how the grain runs in ebony, it is safer to cut a longer piece than is needed and then split a piece off. Plane following the line of the split, then plane an adjacent face in such a way that the two planed surfaces are at right angles to each other. Square the ends to the correct length. Cut the recess in the edge of the front 1mm smaller than the finished saddle. Saw gently, holding the front firmly against the edge of the bench and being careful that the wood does not crack, and cut through the edge and one black and the white of the purfling.

Joining these cuts with straight lines on both sides of the front, cut from the top down along the purfling and from the inside with the front resting in a cradle. Trim the recess until all the purfling is removed and the saddle fits well against the long edge but is a loose fit at the ends. The front may shrink slightly but the ebony never will.

Angle the inner face of the saddle back from the top of the front so that, when the saddle is finished, the top ridge comes in the centre of the width.

The ends slope down and finish flush with the purfling and curve up to the full edge thickness. The under edge may also be rounded, remembering that the saddle is not flat across but follows the outline of the instrument.

be rubbed off, and check the flatness of the ribs again. Adjust the closing cramps to the right width and then, working in a warm place, gently heat the surfaces to be glued and brush glue on to the blocks and linings. Place them exactly on the back and cramp in place.

If any glue is showing remove it with a damp brush and a chisel-shaped piece of softwood. On the inside a small tooth-brush will clean any glue off effectively,

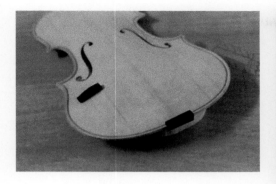

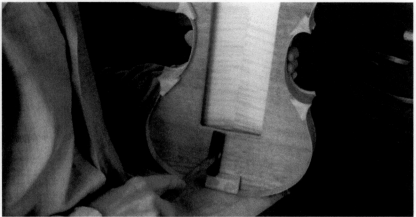

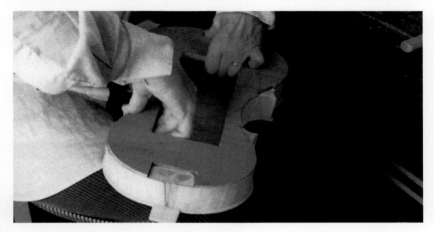

THE MOULD COMES OUT

Now the front is ready to glue on, the time has come to knock out the mould.

Plan your time when removing the mould carefully: the time between removing the mould and gluing on the front should be as short as possible to reduce the possibility of the ribs moving.

Take a small hammer and, resting the block to be hit firmly on a soft surface such as your leg, give it a smart tap on the surface glued to the mould. Repeat this on the remaining five blocks. Then check with a table knife that all the blocks have separated from the mould.

Gently pull the mould up, keeping it parallel to the top edge of the ribs. Now glue in the second set of linings and, when the glue is dry, trim them back on the inside edge and level off the tops, being careful not to remove even a shaving of rib. The corner blocks are gouged down, using the inside ground gouge, gently curving from lining to lining and leaving a little extra thickness where the C-lining is let in, but making them flush with the upper and the lower lining. The gouged surface should be at right angles to the back gluing surfaces and the line round the inside of the instrument made by the shaped blocks and the linings should be a smooth curve. The corners of the end blocks should be well rounded since they do not contribute to the strength of the instrument.

The surfaces of the blocks may be filed, scraped and sandpapered, or, if the tools used were really sharp, left as a chiselled surface.

GLUING ON THE FRONT

Round the inside edge of the front. Then clean the gluing area of the front in the

TOP LEFT: The block for the saddle fitted in place, and a shaped saddle for comparison.

MIDDLE LEFT: Side view of a saddle.

BOTTOM LEFT: Back view of a saddle.

TOP RIGHT: Removing the mould by tapping the blocks with a hammer.

BOTTOM RIGHT: Lifting out the mould, keeping it parallel to the back.

Using a chisel to shape an end block.

Using a file to round the outside edge.

same way that the back was done, and again leave a line where the ribs come at the upper end. Mark half the width of the saddle recess on each side of the centre line on the face of the ribs above the endpin hole. Using these lines, cramp the front in place, this time with four wedged cramping blocks at the ends and check that the overhang is even all the way round. The ends of the corners of the ribs may need to be pushed in a little and their position on the front marked with a pencil dot. When the ribs and front fit perfectly, warm the surfaces to be glued and glue in the same way as the back. If the overhang is uneven, it is possible to push the ribs into a better position before cramping fully. When the glue is dry and the cramps have been removed, warm the saddle well and, putting glue in its recess, push it firmly into place, clean any visible glue off and wait until it is dry.

ROUNDING THE EDGES

A well-rounded edge and an elegant scoop down to the purfling make a great difference to the look of an instrument. In the same way that the undersurfaces of the edges were shaped, the rounding may be done with files or a knife and smoothed with sandpaper. The saddle is rounded along with the rest of the edge; imagine the path the tailgut will take over the saddle and produce a suitable surface to support it.

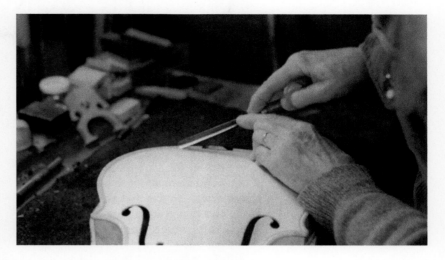

The rounding ends halfway to the purfling. After it is done, sit the body of the instrument in a cradle and clean up the surface from the purfling so that there is a neat ridge where the scoop meets the rounding. The ridge may come exactly halfway between the outside edge and the rounding or fractionally nearer the outside edge. On the back this can be done with a scraper, but on the front it is difficult to scrape across the grain and so the inside curve at the corners, each side of the saddle and the edge where the neck will be let in should be finished with a No. 7 gouge.

Once the neck is fitted it is more difficult to work on the body and so now is the time to check all the surfaces and ensure that they are clean and smooth.

Gouging the fluting from the purfling to the rounded edge.

8 THE SCROLL

INSPECTING THE GRAIN OF THE NECK BLOCK

The neck of the violin will be more stable if the wood from which it is made is cut on the quarter; so the first surface to inspect is the end that will be the root of the neck. To decide which end this will be the following must be considered. If the figure on the sides of the neck block will slope at the same angle as the figure of the ribs it is pleasing, but more important is the grain along the block (*see* photo on page 10). On scrolls there is always a danger of a crack developing from the top peghole to the throat, so try to place the scroll template in such a way that the grain runs either parallel to the fingerboard face of the scroll block or slightly back from it at this point. The grain on the length to which the fingerboard will be glued should be as straight as possible. Having considered the figure on the side of the block and the grain along the fingerboard face, clean up the end that will be the root of the neck so that it is possible to see the end grain. If this is parallel to the fingerboard face it is necessary only to square back the two sides, making the block the correct width. If it is not, see how much you can improve it taking into consideration the widths between the eyes, at the back of the scroll, and where the button will come.

Now plane the fingerboard face and the two sides square to this face and parallel to each other. Having done this, mark out the scroll by using a pencil round the outside and pricking through the holes that mark the volute, though only gently round the

LEFT BELOW: Aligning the fingerboard face of the scroll block to the end grain, taking the widths of the scroll eyes, the back and the button into consideration.

RIGHT BELOW: Planing the fingerboard face of the scroll block.

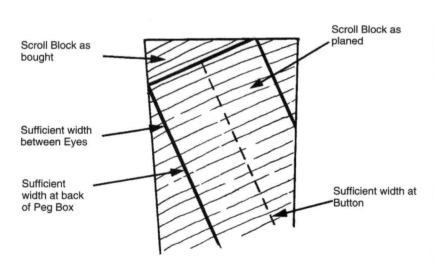

Scroll Block as bought

Sufficient width between Eyes

Sufficient width at back of Peg Box

Scroll Block as planed

Sufficient width at Button

eye. Use a square to check that the scroll is marked on exactly opposite sides of the block. Saw out as accurately as possible, then bevel both sides to the pencil line and tidy the outline with chisel, gouge and files. This will remain the final outline and so should be beautiful.

PEGBOX

The top of the fingerboard should line up with the tail of the scroll, or the top of the hen's tail on cellos. Allow the width of the nut above this point and draw a line across square to the sides of the block. This line marks the beginning of the pegbox, so make a step 0.5mm down from the fingerboard face here, since later, after the instrument has been varnished, it may be necessary to plane a shaving off when refitting the fingerboard to the neck. With a step down there is no danger of removing varnish from the top of the pegbox walls.

Set the pencil marking gauge to half the width of the block and draw a centre line all round the scroll and the neck. With pencil compasses to ensure symmetry,

mark out the pegbox back and front and the contours of the volute, following the measurements and looking at pictures of scrolls. The sides of the front of the pegbox should be very slightly convex, while the sides of the back of the pegbox should remain parallel to the centre line for at least half their length. If drilling the pegholes by hand, it is easiest to locate them now, marking across with a square and following the diagram and measurements.

The distance Z in the diagram below left should be 10mm for violins, 12mm for violas and 15mm for cellos. This allows for the diameter of the peg and a clearance of more than two string thicknessses all round. The top peghole should be central in the width of the pegbox. Draw a line from the point marking the centre of the top peghole to the beginning of the pegbox. The centres of the intermediate pegholes should be located on this line, then strings from the top pegs will not rub on the lower pegs on their path to the nut. If copying an instrument with a very curvy pegbox, the intermediate pegholes may have to be raised in order to leave

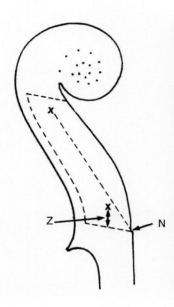

LEFT: Locating the step down to the pegbox.

RIGHT: Drilling the peg holes.

sufficient clearance underneath. For those with access to a press drill the pegholes may be drilled right through later, even after the pegbox has been made. Some makers prefer to varnish with no pegholes – which may collect varnish – and then to make the holes after the instrument is nearly complete.

Cut across by the throat, saw cut 1, to within 1mm of the lines marking the back and the front of the pegbox, and then saw along the sides of the pegbox.

On cello scrolls also mark a line on the side of the scroll, square to the fingerboard face, that joins the top of the fingerboard line to the top of the hen's tail. Cut in on both sides, square to the sides of the scroll block, to 1mm short of the fingerboard width at the front and 1mm short of the width of the hen's tail at the back. Violinists would not like the extra width of the pegbox at this point since it would interfere with their hand position, but it is a much more sensible design which allows the outer strings to run straight back to their pegs. These strings must be placed close to the edge of the fingerboard and yet run into the pegbox (*see* photo on page 102). Occasionally you will find this design on violas – viola players being the more tolerant.

Make saw cut 2 downwards and cut in at the back of the scroll to remove this piece of wood. Every downward saw cut should angle slightly away from the centre. Eventually this will be gouged straight. Cut in at the back of the scroll to remove the piece of wood outside sawcut 2.

Using gouges and the little planes shape the outside of the pegbox and finish with a scraper. The sides should be flat across the width and slightly convex in the length. When the outside is good, mark the width of the walls and cut down with a saw or

Location of saw cuts 1, 2, 3 and 4.

RIGHT: Sawing the sides of the pegbox.

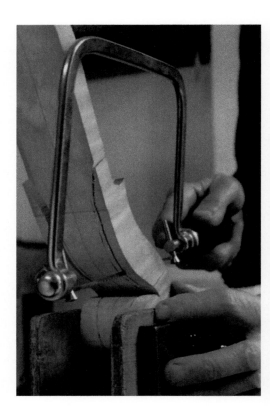

knife, angling the cuts towards each other so that the walls of the pegbox widen as they go down. Drill or gouge out the wood between the cuts and clean up the inside with chisels, taking care at the bottom to leave enough thickness for the fluting that will be made round the scroll.

At the throat the wood is inclined to chip so it is easier to use a round gouge first and then square the corners afterwards.

The bottom of the pegbox must be thicknessed carefully; it is easy to go right through. Under the top peg particularly it should curve up, not go down and through.

VOLUTE
(See illustrations on pp. 66–68)

When the pegbox is finished make saw cuts 3 and 4 down to the pencil line marking the volute and remove these pieces of wood. Turn the square left by saw cuts 2, 3 and 4 into a curve that follows the prick marks by gouging down. Do this on both sides and the remaining piece of wood should look like a large piece of dowel that passes squarely through the middle of the scroll.

Continue the surface that follows on from the sides of the pegbox, keeping the inner surface lower than the outside and cutting with a straight chisel which is less likely to make indentations in the dowel-shaped middle of the scroll.

On this part draw the front and the back view of the volute.

These are the lines that will stop saw cuts 5, 6 and 7 and, with these lines in place, the cuts may be made downwards and sideways to remove three pieces from both sides of the scroll.

Gouge down to the prick marks, again keeping the cuts from both sides lined up across the scroll.

On these surfaces draw the final spiral of the volute and make saw cut 8 and the half cut 9, being careful not to saw right

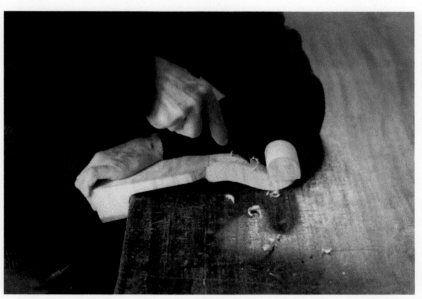

across. The slope down from the eye of the scroll along saw cut 9 may be chiselled away and the wood left by cut 8 sawn away. Finish the back and the front view of the scroll, chiselling the saw cuts into a flowing line. Looked at from the back, the edges of the volute are nearly parallel to the centre line, while looking at the scroll from on top or from the front, the edges of

TOP: Making saw cut 2.

BELOW: Gouging out the pegbox.

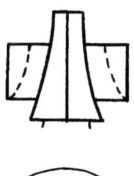

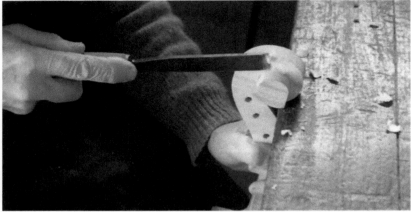

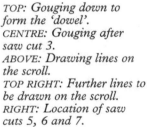

TOP: *Gouging down to form the 'dowel'.*
CENTRE: *Gouging after saw cut 3.*
ABOVE: *Drawing lines on the scroll.*
TOP RIGHT: *Further lines to be drawn on the scroll.*
RIGHT: *Location of saw cuts 5, 6 and 7.*

the volute further from the centre line make curves similar to those nearer to it.

Cut a flat bevel at least 1mm wide on all these edges with a knife and a small chisel held at 45 degrees and continue the bevel all along the pegbox and round the hen's tail,

being careful to cut the right way of the grain.

Now gouge the sides of the scroll, if possible, by gouging both sides in the same way. Sometimes the grain makes it easier to gouge one side from the eye downwards or the pegbox upwards. First cut down round the central 'dowels' then cut in from the bevel towards the centre, being careful to leave the bevel an even width. Gouge deeply at the eye of the scroll and gradually more shallowly until the gouging merges into the pegbox side. Round the eye of the scroll it will be necessary to cut down and gouge in more

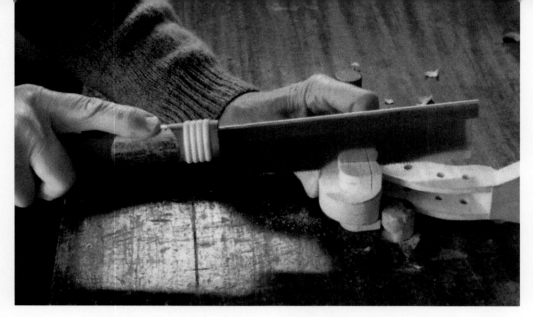

Making saw cut 6.

CENTRE: *Sawing off the wood outside saw cut 6.*

FAR LEFT: *Back view of a scroll.*

BOTTOM LEFT: *Front view of a scroll.*

BELOW: *Location of saw cuts 8 and 9.*

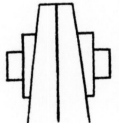

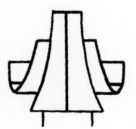

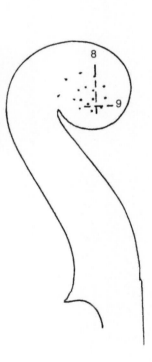

Bevelling the scroll with a knife.

BOTTOM: *Gouging the volute.*

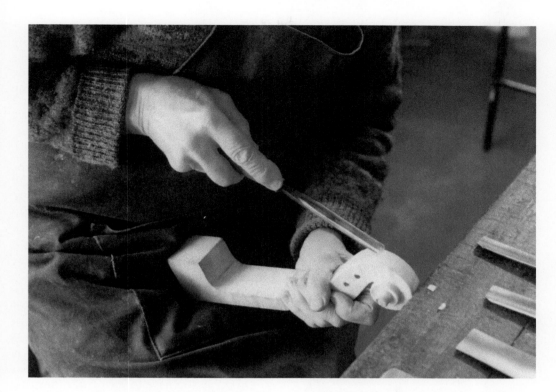

Fluting the back of the scroll.

BELOW: Fluting under the chin of the scroll with a gouge.

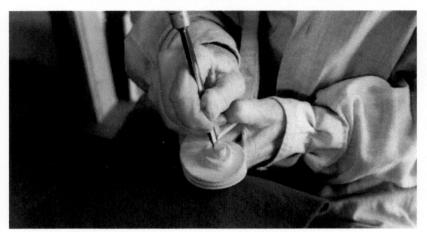

open out the curve of the throat. This may be begun with a small chisel, it is easiest to finish the curve with a half-round needle file, remembering that, if the curve is too open, the likelihood of a crack running up from the top peghole is greater.

FLUTING

The fluting is a gentle scoop from the bevel up to the centre line. With the No. 7 gouge cut a groove next to the bevel all round, but leave the centre line untouched at the hen's tail.

Using wider gouges where the fluting is wider, broaden the groove right up to the centre line from both sides. The scoop should be deeper where the scroll is narrow and shallow where it is wider, especially at the back of the pegbox. Just above the hen's tail there is a difficult area where the grain directions meet and it will be easier to gouge across the grain here. On cellos you have to leave a continuation of the hen's tail bevel. Look at a photograph. When gouging under the chin towards the throat protect the latter with a small spare piece of rib.

Eventually it is easier to finish this part with a knife, cutting across the grain and this technique is also useful around the top of the fluting where the half-round needle file is also a help.

Clean up the eye of the scroll by using the smallest chisel, first cutting gently down, sliding the gouge round the eye, and then cutting in from the bevel.

Using the finger-shaped and egg-shaped scrapers, smooth the fluting, keeping the spine and the edges of the bevel sharp. The small pointed scrapers will smooth the volute, although clean gouge marks if shallow may look attractive.

TOP: *Fluting under the chin of the scroll with a knife.*

CENTRE: *Gouging the eye of the scroll.*

ABOVE: *Using scrapers to smooth the scroll.*

than once. Try to use the same gouging directions on both sides so that the eyes on each side look similar.

THE THROAT

Depending on how accurately the scroll was sawn, it will almost certainly be necessary to

9 SETTING THE NECK

With the body and the scroll of the instrument finished, the time has come to put them together. This is not such a difficult undertaking as many people think so long as each step is carefully taken and lines, heights and measurements are checked often. There is an old carpenter's saying: 'Measure twice, cut once', which is true; it is even safer to measure three times.

FINGERBOARD

First the fingerboard must be made or finally shaped if it is already part-made. If beginning with a rectangular piece of wood, preferably cut between slab and quarter sawn, plane one side perfectly flat and draw a generous outline. Saw it out in such a way that the wood planes well from the narrow end to the wide one on the underside and the other way on the upper face that will be curved. With luck, a part-made fingerboard will work in these directions too.

Plane the sides smooth, keeping them at right angles to the flat side and distinctly concave. If a straight edge is held along the side there should be a dip down to a generous millimetre in the middle. Players find that this helps them to shift into high positions, and it has the added advantage that, since the upper surface is also concave along its length, the edge thickness remains constant. After the fingerboard has been planed to the correct widths, draw a centre line and check that the ends are square to it, or check the angles with a bevel. If necessary, file the ends, always working in from the edges and keeping the ends square to the flat

side. At the wide end the end grain should be smoothed by using sandpaper glued to blocks of wood which will also be useful finally to polish the curved surface.

It is worth making a template to the

TOP: Planing the underside of the fingerboard flat.

BOTTOM: Planing the sides of the fingerboard.

correct width of the fingerboard and with a curve of the correct radius at the wide end. At the narrow end the curve should be a little flatter. Most cellists like a flat surface, known as a Romberg after the first cellist to demand it, under the lowest string. Scratch the edge width of the fingerboard along the sides and plane a bevel down to the scratch line. Checking with the template and the straight edge, shape the top curve.

The concavity in the length of the fingerboard should be less under the upper string, which is always at a higher tension. Eventually the curved surface of the fingerboard must be filed along its length without rounding down the ends, scraped and sandpapered to a fine finish; but, as even ebony may move, the final polishing may be left until the instrument is varnished and the fingerboard reglued to the neck. However, the underside of the fingerboard may be finished. It will look more elegant if a slope is planed from the

place where the neck ends, approximately half the length of the fingerboard, to the wide end, where the edge width may be made 1mm thinner.

On this surface draw a semi-circle of radius 2mm less than half the width of the fingerboard, so that the curve is 10mm away from the end of the neck point, and continue a line 2mm away from the edge along each side. Gouge down definitely on the semicircle line and hollow out the underside of the fingerboard, particularly along the edges which contribute less to its strength. The profile of the hollowing at the wide end should be parallel to the top curve. Smooth all the hollowing with the smallest plane, scrapers and sandpaper.

GLUING THE NECK TO THE FINGERBOARD

On the surface of the neck reinforce the centre line at the top of the fingerboard with a compass-point hole deep enough to

RIGHT: Checking the fingerboard curve with the template.

LEFT: The area on the underside of the fingerboard to be hollowed.

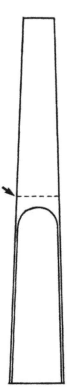

survive when this surface is planed smooth. Test this surface on your flat surface, taking care that it remains square to the sides of the neck block. Mark half the width of the top of the fingerboard on each side of the compass-point mark and cramp the fingerboard in place using the fingerboard cramping block. Put a straight edge against both edges of the fingerboard, holding them up past the scroll and check that the straight edges are symmetrical on each side of the centre line of the scroll. If they are not, keep the fingerboard in the centre of the neck at the peg-box but manoeuvre the other end until the alignment improves. When it is as good as possible draw a line on the neck along the sides of the fingerboard, uncramp it and draw a new centre line equidistant from these two new lines.

Decide how deeply you want to let the neck into the body, remembering that the depth at the button will be greater than at the front; this angle resists the pull of the strings better. It looks neat if the neck is let in just through the purfling, but it may go in deeper. Measure the chosen depth from the top edge of the front and add this measurement to the neck stop. Mark this total distance down from the top of the fingerboard line, *not* from the pegbox, and draw a line on the fingerboard face of the neck at right angles to the centre line, and a line on the side of the neck back 87° (85° for cellos).

Saw off any superfluous length and plane the base of the neck from the fingerboard edge back towards the button to a perfectly flat surface.

Making the base and the sides of the neck perfect makes the setting of the neck easier. End grain works more easily if slightly damp, but remember to clean your plane blade at the end of the operation.

The sides of the neck may be sawn off now or removed later. Attach the fingerboard to the neck with three small

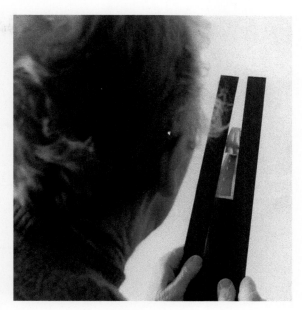

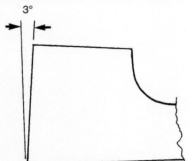

3°

Checking the alignment of the fingerboard and the scroll.

The root should be cut at 87°.

spots of glue and, when this is dry, draw a centre line on the base of the neck. Add the distance from the fingerboard to the front, the thickness of the front, the rib height and also the back thickness (since the taper of the sides of the neck will continue through the back thickness). At this point mark the button width.

Draw a line from the sides of the fingerboard to the width of the button, continuing the line past the button if there is extra wood. The root of the neck ends where the back joins the ribs; but fitting the neck is easier if there is extra wood. Gouge the sides of the neck away from the edge of the fingerboard,

RIGHT: *How to work out the shape of the root of the neck.*

BOTTOM: *Planing the sides of the neck root.*

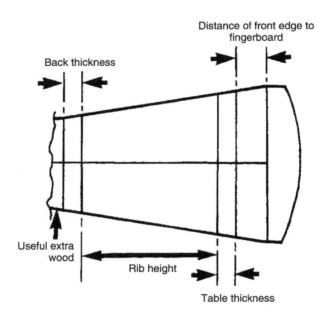

Distance of front edge to fingerboard

Back thickness

Useful extra wood

Rib height

Table thickness

following the line drawn on the base of the neck at the root and maintaining this angle along the sides of the neck. Since it is difficult to work on a cello neck once it has been set into the body, it is wise to hollow the area near the pegbox between the hen's tail and the fingerboard now. File the sides of the neck level with the fingerboard and then plane the root of the neck.

As this is the surface which will be let into the body, it must be flat and the slope of the sides must follow the fingerboard width.

On both sides of the neck at the root draw a short line parallel to the fingerboard at the distance away from the fingerboard that the front edge will finally come (pencil line A). From the point where the top of the fingerboard meets the neck, measure down to line A the neck stop length and at this point draw a line towards the button parallel to the base of the neck (pencil line B).

FITTING THE NECK TO THE BODY

Measure the width of the root of the neck at line A and, on the top ribs, mark half this width, minus 1mm on both sides, equidistant from the centre line where the ribs meet the front. Where the ribs and the back meet, mark half the button width again less 1mm on both sides. Then join these marks with a pencil line on the ribs. Sit the root of the neck on the ribs, away from the button, and check that the angles you have just drawn are similar to the angles of the sides of the neck. If the angles match, cut along the line with a fine saw and/or a knife. Eventually the recess will stop at the inside purfling line, but for now leave one purfling black uncut. Do not saw too deeply. When all the rib has been cut right through, cut the edge of the front crossways and then chisel back the ribs and some of the top block.

Using a bevel to check the sides of the root.

LEFT: *Location of line A and line B.*

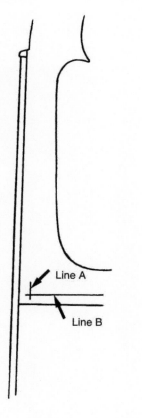

Line A

Line B

As the base of the recess is end grain on the front edge and side grain on the block, it is easiest to cut the end grain across with a knife and the block back with a chisel.

Along the sides of the recess the ends of the ribs may be chiselled; but to chisel the sides of the block would cause it to split, so from the rib edge the block must be cut downwards with a knife or a chisel, being careful not to leave a bump where rib and block meet and not to undercut.

When line A is still 10mm away from the front on both sides concentrate on the base only ➤ pencil line B must eventually touch the top edge of the front ➤ the base of the recess must be free from bumps and wobbles, and ➤ angled so that the fingerboard points straight down the instrument ➤. If the elevation stick is placed over the bridge line, the distance between the foot of the elevation stick and the front should equal the distance from the top edge of the front to pencil line A.

Continue working on the base of the recess until these four aims have been achieved. Now work on the sides of the recess. Keep the centre joint of the back in the middle and check that the distance from the fingerboard to the front is the same on both sides of the fingerboard. It is essential that the sides of the recess should fit the sides of the neck root all the way down and that the end of the root fits the button.

If there is a lot of surplus wood to remove from the end of the root it helps to remove some now. Fit the neck into the recess and draw a line on the root 2–3mm beyond its eventual end with a ruler held at right angles to the ribs. Having taken the neck out, draw a line at the same place across the base of the neck parallel to the fingerboard and saw this piece off.

Plane the end of the root only when it touches the button. Having carefully marked where it touches, either cramp the neck down in the fingerboard cramping

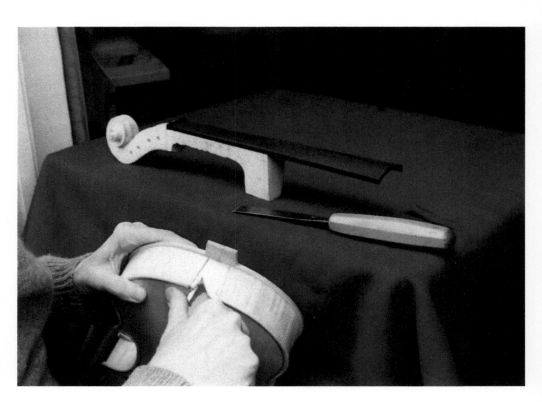

Beginning the recess in the body: cutting the front edge.

Beginning the recess in the body: chiselling back.

Beginning the recess in the body: cutting the side with a knife.

Checking the alignment of the fingerboard on the bridge.

RIGHT: Checking the elevation.

block to the bench or hold the scroll against the padded edge of the bench and, taking great care, plane a flat surface. On violins and violas an even gap of 0.5mm can be left between the root and the button and it will cramp up, but on cellos the gap should be negligible. When testing the fit or when gluing in the neck, the body should be held against the bench (*see* photo opposite above). Before gluing in the neck, cramp it up and, having checked the elevation and that the fingerboard is pointing at the bridge, put a pencil line across both the button and the neck that will demonstrate, after the neck has been glued in, that the neck is back in exactly the same position. Remove the neck and size the base with very thin glue, then warm all surfaces, apply glue, push the neck into the recess and cramp in, fastening the cramp up firmly.

Wash off any visible glue, having checked the alignment and the pencil line.

THE NUT

Shape a piece of ebony to fit between the pegbox and the fingerboard. It should be at least 2mm higher than the fingerboard, and widen from the width of the fingerboard to the width of the pegbox. The face next to the pegbox should slope back at approximately 80 degrees. Glue it lightly to the end of the fingerboard only.

SHAPING THE NECK

If players are not happy with the shape of the neck, they will not be happy with the instrument, so this must be done carefully. First trim the sides of the button to form a continuation of the sides of the neck root, leaving extra wood near the ribs. Now continue the edges of the back towards the button, removing this extra wood and keeping the edge of the back parallel to the

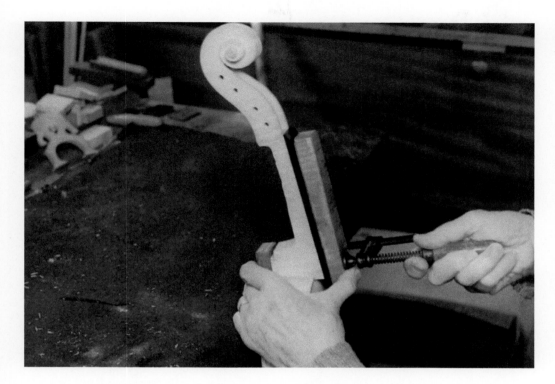

Cramping the neck in place.

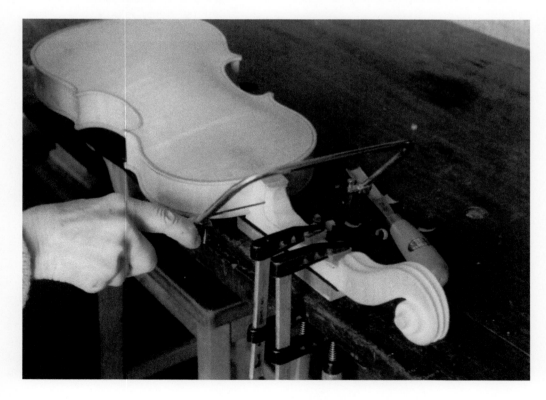

Sawing down by the button and round the curve of the neck.

*Cutting the root on the
bass side with a knife.*

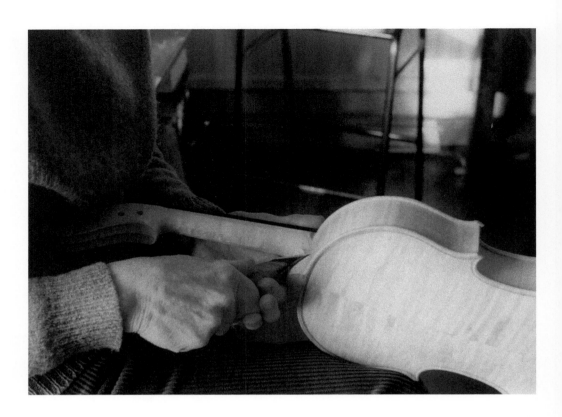

*Cutting the root on the
treble side with a knife.*

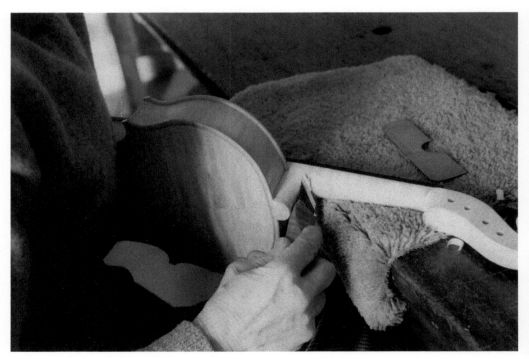

purfling. Draw a semi-circle with its centre equidistant from the sides of the button and 2mm above an imaginary continuation of the edge of the back across the button. Draw a line across the top of the semi-circle and put a mark at each end on the sides of the button. Measure the upper and the lower thickness of the neck and the fingerboard and subtract the finished thickness and mark the difference in from the edge of the neck. For example, if the present neck thickness is 24mm and it should be 19mm, mark 5mm in on the side of the neck. Using the neck template, of which there is a scaled-down drawing with the workshop templates on page 16, draw in the finished curve, joining the top of the button line and the two thickness lines. On cellos a fourth point is necessary: at 70mm back from the fingerboard the height of the root should be 30mm. Saw down just outside this line from the button, with the neck firmly cramped on the fingerboard cramping block and to the bench (*see* bottom photo on page 79).

It is easier and safer to gouge across rather than along the neck. Use a knife round the sides of the button and the sides of the neck.

Where the root curve and the neck curve meet, the sides must curve in; and similarly at the transition from the hen's tail to the nut, the neck also curves in, nearly up to the lower peghole. Having used the knife to shape both ends of the neck, it is possible to shape the sides with a small spokeshave, remembering, however, that this tool has a tendency to make

surfaces hollow. The sides of the neck must be straight. The edge of the neck template or a small square is useful for checking this. Smooth the neck with files, working mainly along the grain and carry the rounding on through half the edge width of the fingerboard. Check the curves with the neck template. The outer edge of the fingerboard and the nut should also be rounded, making the widest part of the neck curve halfway across the thickness of the fingerboard edge. The player's hand is rounded round the neck and does not want to feel sharp edges or too much wood along the sides but an almost elliptical curve instead. Scrape and sandpaper until the neck is completely smooth.

Scraping the root of the neck.

10 VARNISHING

Violin makers used to refer to 'oil varnish' or 'spirit varnish' and at one time spirit varnish had a bad reputation for being too hard. It is true that varnish should be neither hard nor sticky as both inhibit vibrations, but that depends more on the resins used than on the solvent, and a so-called spirit varnish may contain oil. However, the names are so convenient that they will be used throughout this chapter.

MAKING SPIRIT VARNISH

The big advantages of spirit varnish are that each coat is so thin that the final thickness of the complete varnish is small and it dries quickly. The big disadvantage is that each coat immediately dissolves the previous one, so varnish must be brushed on swiftly and you must never brush the same area twice except to catch a run. If butyl alcohol is used the varnish dries more slowly and is slightly easier to spread, but there is still the danger of having too thin a varnish or varnish containing a little water running into furrows or becoming pock-marked. Spirit varnish can be bought but it is easy to make. Keep to a ratio of 25g of resin to 100ml alcohol, with the possible addition of 5ml of essential oil, such as rosemary oil or even castor oil. A half-and-half mix of hard resins (sticklack, copal or colophonium) and soft resins (mastic and sandarac, both fairly soft or benzoin and elemi, both very soft) works well. Fine natural colours such as dragon's blood, or a lake made by heating, for example, pernambuco shavings in water and then letting the water evaporate, will easily dissolve in alcohols.

MAKING OIL VARNISH

Nowadays many makers use a so-called 'Fulton varnish' – named after the man who was first enthusiastic about it and wrote down the recipe. It can be bought, but is difficult to make. It must be made out of doors because of the smell and fire risk. If you want to try, weigh an aluminium saucepan, take 20g of sandarac and thoroughly melt; add, one-third at a time, 80g of rosin ww pale quality, taking the temperature up to 340°C. Test for colour on a tile – the longer it is heated the darker the colour but the smaller the yield. Weigh the saucepan and its contents; the resins may now weigh only 30g. Allow to cool to 150°. Preheat alkali-refined linseed oil to 100° and add less than an equal weight for undercoat, equal quantities for the main coats and one-and-a-half times the weight for the last coat. Heat to 300° until a 50–75mm thread can be pulled from a drop on a tile. Filter through a cloth and store in the dark in a well-sealed bottle. Add turpentine to thin for use. (It is safer to buy this varnish.)

The remainder of this chapter consists of my son's notes on the use of bought varnish, interspersed with my ideas on other methods.

WHY DO WE VARNISH INSTRUMENTS?

The main considerations are appearance and preservation. A white instrument will get dirty quickly and come unglued frequently. Sweat from the player will damage the wood too. Applying some varnish will immediately produce more depth of figure in the wood and, as there are many varnishes available and many colours to add to them, it is also a way of giving your instrument a distinctive look.

EQUIPMENT

Brushes

Synthetic hair brushes are suitable for use with oil varnish, for instance, 'Prolene by Pro Arte'. For violins and violas you will need a 25mm brush for the body and a 12mm one for the scroll, and for cellos, 40mm and 25mm ones. These should always be cleaned in genuine turpentine – never detergents nor white spirit. Artists' quality distilled turpentine should be used for thinning the varnish.

In order that spirit varnish can be put on quickly, wider brushes are needed – 50mm for the back and the front and 25mm for the ribs and the scroll; they should be thicker to hold more varnish, but well squeezed out to avoid runs. A little purple in methylated spirits causes no harm, but butyl alcohol is an equally good solvent. Never push the brushes down into the solvent container because this may cause the bristles to break and they may come out when varnishing. If this does happen, remove the bristle with the tip of a knife, either at once or, if that is difficult, after the varnish is dry.

Oil Varnish

When buying the varnish it is essential to buy clear varnish and, in addition, golden brown varnish and possibly red varnish. It is possible to buy clear varnish with more or less linseed oil. You can use a stiffer, harder varnish at the start and then move to a more flexible one, but not the other way round, and to use a flexible varnish throughout is possible. It is easier to use coloured varnish than to add colour. The extracts that are sold come in a liquid medium and increase the volatility of the varnish mixture to a degree where it sets too quickly for it to be possible to spread it evenly. Some artists' oil colours are truly transparent; madder – also called alizarin – burnt umber and burnt sienna are reasonably so. However, one cannot tell exactly what is in the tube with the colour and these other components may affect the robustness of the varnish and make the final drying process slow and even permanently soften the varnish.

As well as varnish, solvent, colour and brushes, materials for rubbing down are needed. After every coat from the second onwards the varnish must be rubbed down by using linseed oil and 1200 grit wet and dry paper, and kitchen towels. Rubbing down is important since it helps the next coat to key on; it will spread better on a smooth surface and the oil residue will also help the next coat to spread.

Storage

Oil varnish must be kept in small jars in the dark since it is light-reactive. Larger jars, for instance, one-pound honey or jam jars, will be needed for holding the varnish to be applied and for washing the brushes. For spirit varnish a pudding basin is better

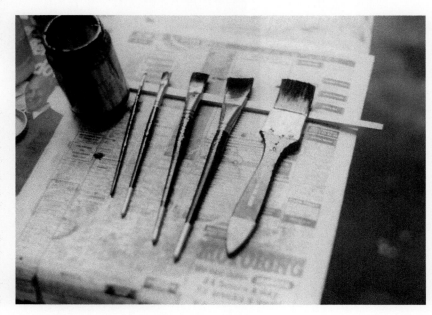

Varnish brushes and a varnish jar with a nylon line across the top.

and a line across the top, similar to that on the glue pot, is needed to wipe the brushes on.

DRYING

Sunlight is good, but dust-free and fly-free sunlight is rare and, unless the instrument can rotate freely, the heat may cause glued joints to come open. A dust-free room is slow: a UV cabinet is practical. A box fitted with type 4005, 40W, polymer fluorescent UV tubes, an extractor fan and a thermostat are needed with space around the instrument. The thermostat should be set no higher than 22°C and a pot of water should be kept in the box to prevent the instrument from drying out. It is still possible for an instrument to come unstuck and so always check the gluing before rubbing down and applying the next coat.

A violin with false fingerboard, hook and string around the neck.

CLEANING UP

Having assembled the necessary equipment, the instrument must be prepared for varnishing. All good varnishing results come from good cleaning up. First the fingerboard must be removed. If it does not come off easily by lifting the wide end, cautiously insert a thin table knife and pop it off. It must be replaced by a block of softwood covering the neck completely and attached to it with three small spots of glue. So that this may be removed easily, leave a gap for the knife at one corner. Otherwise it should fit the neck perfectly and so prevent it from warping. The block will also take a hook by which the instrument may be hung up and it is wise to tie a piece of string round the neck below the hook just in case the glue fails.

Begin by cleaning the ribs and the rounded edges of the back and the front. This may be done with sandpaper; persevere, until the edges are really smooth curves all the way round, using a narrow, folded piece of sandpaper along the edge. The back and the front should be scraped with a very sharp scraper; the back may be sanded with very fine paper. But the front should not be, with a possible exception; before scraping the front you may gently sandpaper six areas:

- the four corner areas;
- above the saddle; and
- below the neck.

These are the problem areas but they should be scraped after sanding. If the front were to be sanded all over, the soft grain would be rubbed away and the hard grain would obtrude. If the front is scraped the soft grain is compressed and the hard lines cut away so that the varnish accentuates the grain. The scroll should be scraped if necessary and may be lightly sanded. All the bevels should be trimmed with cutting tools and, if they have not already been done, the outside walls of the pegbox should be bevelled, along with the button, thus accentuating its circular shape. The fluting round the edges of the back and the front should be gouged across the grain and gouged and/or scraped along the grain, from the purfling up to the rounding of the edge, as shown on page 61.

To summarise, the order of the clean up should be

- edges and ribs (sandpaper);
- back and front (mainly scraper and a little sandpaper);
- scroll (files, scrapers and sandpaper); and
- bevels and fluting (cutting tools).

After cleaning, try to get all the dust out of the instrument. Also prepare a piece of spruce and one of maple to experiment and try out colours on.

STAINING AND SIZING

If stained, figured maple may lose much of its beauty. The stain sinks more into the pores of the wood and on the sides of the waves, which then turn into dull stripes instead of having movement in them. Spruce stains unevenly since the stain sinks in more at the top and the bottom of the front where the fibres of the wood are cut. This happens less if the instrument is rubbed with silica gel 60, either dry or suspended in colourless alcohol – not mixed with water because this would raise the grain. It is basically a filler with the correct refractive index. Oil does not bond well to waterglass or casein and so these are not recommended as grain fillers. Spirit varnish bonds better to other substances, and wood prepared with a medieval mayonnaise using egg yolk, a little linseed oil, propolis (bee resin dissolved in alcohol) fig sap and other exciting ingredients can look attractive, be sweat resistant and bond to spirit varnish. Before using oil varnish, a very little oil

Using a knife to bevel the button.

colour mixed with turpentine may be brushed on to kill the whiteness of the wood and stronger colour may be put on the neck which will not be varnished. If you are going to stain the front, brush it twice with pure turpentine before quickly using the weak stain. Varnish, put direct on to wood polished with silica gel, makes an acceptable ground.

APPLYING OIL VARNISH

Always begin varnishing with clear coats. The first purpose of these is to prevent any pigment in the colour coats from sinking into the wood. The other is to improve further the smoothness of the main surfaces so that the colour coats may be applied more evenly. There is another advantage: clear coats are practice for the colour ones. The varnish may need to be diluted. Brush marks should spread to a smooth surface and the varnish should be easy to brush, so try it out first on the experimental pieces of wood. The first coat can be thicker and will dry more quickly as the air will reach it from both sides. Once the surface is sealed the air acts only on the outer surface.

RIGHT: Brush directions for varnishing, stage A.

The worst thing you can do is to put on another coat before the previous one is dry; if you do, the previous coat will never dry.

Apply the varnish somewhere where there is good natural light and which is warm and free from dust. A piece of dowel half the length of the instrument's back and tapered to fit the endpin hole can support the instrument. When drying, violins and violas may be hung from the hook in the false fingerboard, but cellos are too heavy for this and should be supported on a floor-mounted pin going into the endpin hole.

After the first coat, the pegbox and the f-holes may be left unvarnished and finished later with black varnish, or they may be varnished with the rest of the instrument; be particularly careful not to get runs coming down from the f-holes.

Using the brushes suggested, you will need to dip deeply into the varnish and then wipe the brush on the string across the jar top dipping about three times for the back, three for the front, once for each rib and three times for the scroll. When varnishing the back and the front it is not necessary to wipe the brush so hard. Always brush finally with the figure of the back, the grain of the front and along the ribs.

- Start with the back and its edges, not forgetting the button.
- Then the front and its edges, varnishing the f-holes first if they are not to be blackened.
- Then the ribs, the top two first and the root of the neck – about 25mm up towards the scroll. Then the lower half of the C-curves, inverting the instrument on to its scroll for varnishing the upper curve; then the lower ribs may be varnished, with the instrument held this way up and also, with only a little vanish in the brush, the base of the neck above the front.

Turn the instrument upright and varnish the scroll. In more detail the procedure is the following.

THE BACK

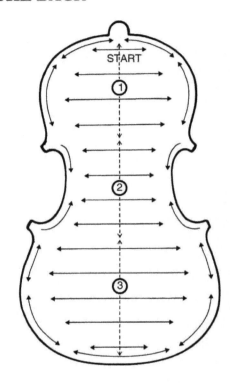

Stage A. From start (1), apply varnish, moving left or right down to the level of the upper corners, then brush around the top (button included) from one upper corner to the other. From (2), follow the same routine to the line of the lower corners. Brush round the C-bout from corner to corner. Then (3), go to the bottom edge, run round the lower bouts from lower corner to endpin on both sides.
Stage B. Making sure that the brush is nearly dry, follow the arrows, starting at (1), going in one stroke from top to bottom, then, also all in one stroke, follow (2) through to (11).
Stage C. Applying virtually no pressure at all, brush, from either edge, from the line of the purfling to the opposite purfling in

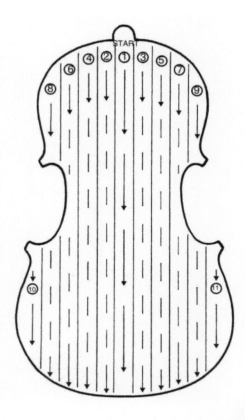

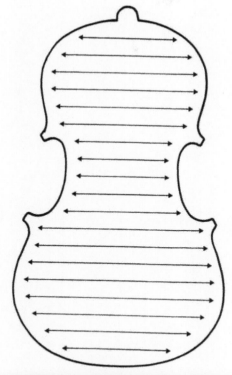

LEFT: Brush directions for varnishing, stage B.

RIGHT: Brush directions for varnishing, stage C.

one stroke, working from top to bottom.
Stage D. Finally, holding the brush at 90 degrees to the edge in the plane of the ribs, pull from inside to outside to cover the outside edge.

THE FRONT

Diagrams A, C, B and D show the sequence for the front.

Stage A. As for the back.
Stage C. As for the back – pretend that the f-holes are not there.
Stage B. As for the back – again pretend that the f-holes are not there.
Stage D. You may get small runs from the f-holes in the positions marked * after A, C and B; further brushing may be necessary in the directions shown.

Varnishing the back.

Brushing out 'runs' from the f-holes, stage D.

RIGHT: Varnishing the front.

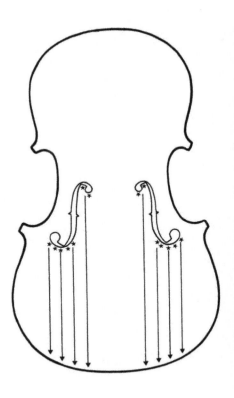

THE RIBS AND THE HEEL OF THE NECK

Start with the upper left or right rib, brush from the neck to the corner and then go over it as many times as you need to in either direction in order to obtain an even finish. Never brush sideways. Then cover the heel of the neck, finishing in the line of the figure and then the other top rib. Then varnish the C-ribs from near the top corner to the lower corner. You will not be able to see all of the C-rib to be able to do it all in one operation, so we have to join up the two halves and this must be done reasonably quickly. To complicate matters, the instrument has to be turned over between doing the two halves. Once

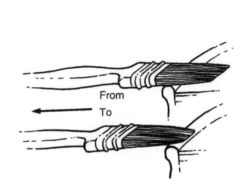

Brush directions for varnishing ribs, stage E.

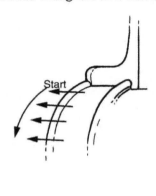

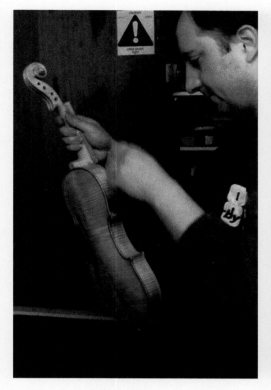

LEFT: *Varnishing a rib with the instrument supported on its peg.*

Varnishing a rib with the instrument supported on its scroll.

varnish is on all but the part around the upper corner on both ribs put the brush down across the top of the jar and turn the instrument over *with the f-holes facing upwards*. This is to prevent any dust still inside the instrument from coming out through the holes. Then, *without putting any more varnish on the brush*, draw the varnish that is there round to the tip of the upper corner. Watch that the corner does not act like the string on the jar and produce a run from the edge. Finally, varnish from the endpin to the lower corner on each side and the little protuberance of the neck over the edge of the front.

THE SCROLL

You should now be using the smaller brush and using less varnish on it. Start with the back of the pegbox and brush upwards over the top of the scroll and round to below the chin. Then dip again and do the sides of the pegbox up to the throat. Return to the back of the pegbox and brush over it repeatedly until a satisfactory evenness is obtained. Then go round the volute on both sides. Return to the sides of the pegbox and brush over these from back to front or from front to back until evenness is obtained. Finally brush over the tops of the pegbox walls, as in the style of stage E. It is important to note that, if you are doing the inside of the pegbox with the same varnish as the remainder of the instrument, then this should be done before any other part of the scroll.

WHAT TO DO WHEN THINGS GO WRONG

This is potentially the most important part of the chapter! Here is a list of tips to enable you to retrieve any situation.

Varnishing the scroll.

have too much colour in your varnish or took too long in spreading it. Dip the brush in the rinsing turpentine and brush over the back/front to soften the last layer. After a short while the varnish will loosen to an extent where it can be spread again.

That didn't work
Do the same again, but take some kitchen towel and wipe off all the varnish and start again.

Total disaster: the varnish sets as soon as the brush lands on the surface of the back
There is far too much colour in the varnish. When this happens it is always possible to remove all the varnish with a commercial stripper and start again.

There is one small spot where the varnish will not stick
Rub it down as usual, but wipe over this area very lightly with a cloth that has a small amount of methylated spirits in it. Too much of this or too much pressure and you will start to take off the varnish. The less well dried the previous coat is, the more likely it is that this treatment will be dangerous. It is also affected by the softness of the varnish. See the section on colour extracts.

I get more runs from the f-holes than I can cope with
There is too much residue built up in the tightest sections of the f-holes. Take a scalpel blade and cut away the residue before applying the next coat.

I cannot get enough colour around the inside edges of the back and the front
You can mix up a stronger colour by adding some burnt sienna or burnt umber to a tiny amount of the varnish and use a fine brush to apply an extra coat on the inside edges.

When there's too much varnish on the back or the front
You should have a table next to you with your pots, brushes, linseed oil, barrier cream and such like on it. If it is covered in a layer of newspaper opened out and twelve to fifteen sheets thick, you can always wipe the brush on the newspaper to get rid of an excess of varnish before brushing over the back or the front again.

Small drips or blobs near the edges or round the f-holes
Never, ever use the brush for these; use your fingertip and just make contact with the blob. A well-trained finger is very useful.

Disaster on the back or the front
This may occur where the brushing has started to pull the varnish around rather than spread it evenly. This means that you

BRUSH MAINTENANCE

Since the varnish is light-reactive, it is important to keep the brushes clean and soft between coats. Once you have finished a coat and poured the surplus varnish back into the storage jar and put it away from the light, pour the rinsing turpentine from the other jar into your varnish jar (the one with the fishing line across it) and, with all the brushes in it, swill it around for a while. Then pour most of the turpentine back into the first jar, but leaving about a half-inch depth of it in the varnish jar. Then leave the brushes like that until the next time. Never use detergents to clean a brush. It does not work and may put bubbles into the varnish.

If you are leaving a brush unused for a long time or it becomes cased in a large amount of residue, a jar with cellulose thinners in it will soon soften the brush and thoroughly clean it. You must rinse it in turpentine before using it again. Brushes do not, of course, last forever and they may start to curl slightly in time from being left in a jar resting on their tips.

RUBBING DOWN

This is one of the most important aspects of varnishing. All of the really crucial work is done at the beginning between the application of the clear coats. The first one that you put on will sink into the wood so much that you will not see any shine on the surface after it is dry; there is therefore no point in rubbing down this first coat. The second coat can go straight on with no preparation of the surface. But once this coat is dry we need to think about rubbing down.

Why Do We Rub Down?

There are several good reasons for rubbing down each coat of varnish before applying the next one. The most obvious one will be apparent if an insect lands on your drying instrument and gets stuck. There are also brush or other hairs, specks of dust and so on to remove as best you can from the surface. Furthermore, by rubbing down the surface thousands of tiny scratches are put on it and this process helps the next coat to key on better to the previous one. Lastly, the lubricant used with the abrasive paper in rubbing down leaves a little residue behind on the surface which will help the next coat to spread evenly and give you a little more brushing time.

How Do We Rub Down?

You will need some linseed oil and some 1200 grit wet and dry paper. *Linseed oil and turpentine are carcinogenic so use barrier cream on your hands.* Spread a small amount of the oil over the back, front or ribs and then rub the surface with the paper. Always fold your paper into three so that when folded it measures about 100mm × 50mm. The feel of the surface will change quite quickly after rubbing, from a very grippy, slightly lumpy surface to a smooth, near frictionless one. There are no real problems about overdoing the rubbing on the initial, clear coats since it will not show much; but you must be careful when rubbing down after colour coats not to do too much and start to remove the colour. Of course, there are problems with not doing enough either so it is difficult to judge it correctly. Suffice it to say, that the better made and better cleaned-up an instrument is, the easier it is to varnish and rub it down to a satisfactory result.

When you are rubbing down the instrument you should rub, between each coat, some of the oil residue collected from the back or the front into the neck, leaving it to dry like the varnish.

After a third clear coat has been applied then it is *essential to do the major rubbing down*. This is to make the surfaces of the

Violins and violas drying.

attractive. It is, of course, possible to do too much rubbing down at any stage in the colour coat process, so constant observation of what you are doing is essential.

Assuming that the essential rubbing down has been completed to a nearly perfect surface, then it is possible that so much varnish may have been rubbed off that another clear coat is necessary. This is hard to judge, so, if you are in doubt, then apply another clear coat before putting any colour on. The only advice it is possible to offer is to say that, if the whole instrument was shiny before you rubbed down, then it probably is not too important. The areas to look at are the end grain of the front (below the neck and above the saddle) and the neck root. If these are as shiny as the rest then you are probably safe.

COLOUR COATS

Try the colour varnish on the experimental wood. It takes several coats of colour to achieve any depth of one colour and normally we shall change the colour at certain points too. If you look at old violins where the varnish has to some extent been worn away you will invariably see a range of colours at different points. So it would seem logical that most violins are varnished with a variety of colours stage by stage. It is also true that different colours have different refractive indices and so, by combining different colours layer on layer, the total refractive effect is greater than with only the one colour. The varnish will have the appearance of more depth. Once the desired colour has been achieved, the instrument may be left or given a coat of finishing varnish. Allow at least six weeks for the varnish to harden properly.

back and the front, and the ribs to a lesser extent, absolutely smooth. It is the front which invariably needs the most work. If you look at the front you will see that it has ridges between the grain lines and is slightly corrugated. The first three coats of varnish have filled in these ridges to a degree, and so, when rubbing down, you will be taking a lot more from the higher grain than from the lower. You should aim now to even out this ridge effect completely. After rubbing for a while, wipe away the oily residue from the surface with a kitchen towel and hold the instrument under an artificial light source. Tilt it backwards and forwards in the light and you will see little streaks of shiny surface still present. If they have all gone then you have done enough.

The procedure for the back is different only in as much as the shiny parts left will be in the form of little pools rather than long, thin streaks between the grain lines. This evening out of the surface is important because, if there are still high and low spots on the surface, when you come to rub down after a colour coat, then you will be taking off all the colour from the high spots before rubbing the low spots at all. A pinstriped front does not look

FINISHING

f-holes and Pegbox

Before the instrument can be rubbed down a decision must be made about how to finish the f-holes and the pegbox. If you used the varnish to do the edges of the f-holes and the pegbox then you may ignore this section. If not, you will notice that there is an uneven residue of varnish around the edges of the f-holes; you should take a thin blade and cut away as much of this residue as you dare. Then take a jar of spirit varnish, clear or yellow, and apply some to the edges, particularly around the holes and the wing, all except the long, straighter sections. Once this is dry (10 minutes or so), mix up some spirit black. This is a small quantity of spirit varnish with some black powder added and thinned a little with methylated spirits. Suitable powders include Spirit Black, Aniline Black or soot. Apply the black with a small brush around the f-holes. Any spillage over the edges may be wiped off with a cloth dampened with methylated spirits. Alternatively, mix up a spirit colour which closely matches the finished instrument. This requires the use of an opaque powder colour to permit good coverage in one coat. Try using a yellow ochre powder or a darker one if the instrument is dark. Finish the inside of the pegbox in a similar fashion, sealing the bottom well with pale spirit varnish before using the black.

Last Rub Down and Polishing

You will need some 3200 grit or thereabouts of Micro-Mesh, some Vienna chalk mixed with mineral oil, small pieces of an old sheet and an old toothbrush. For the polishing you will need yet more old sheet and some violin polish. First rub over all of the instrument with the Micro-Mesh, as you would for a normal rub down, until all the shine has gone. You must not rub over the edges, round the volute nor fluting of the scroll. This is done afterwards with the chalk/oil mix. There exist polishing packs with a variety of grades of Micro-Mesh and a very useful foam block for wrapping it round,

which is perfect for the ribs, except for the C-bout. All but the edges of the plates, from the purfling outwards, the ribs and the sides of the pegbox should be dull now. Mix the chalk and the oil into a thick, brown paste in a jar and, with the toothbrush, scrub with it over the edges, round the purfling line and the inside edges of the ribs and round the scroll. *Wear an apron.*

Take a piece of sheet folded into four and mop up all the oil/chalk residue and rub over all of the instrument with the saturated cloth (if it is not saturated then you did not use enough with the toothbrush) for about 15 minutes. Finally, take a fresh cloth to clean the surfaces and polish with violin polish using a piece of sheet folded into four. Hold it over the top of the pot of polish and tilt to get a small amount on to the sheet. Rub vigorously with it over the surfaces of the instrument and then wipe off with a clean duster. It should look really nice now!

USING SPIRIT VARNISH

Spirit varnish is applied in a similar way to oil varnish but more rapidly. The brush strokes must never overlap and, since there can be no further brushing to even the colour out, the brush should move before touching the instrument and land gently in exactly the right place. After softening the brushes in alcohol dry them on kitchen paper. It should be possible to varnish the back with the brush dipped only once into the varnish.

On the front, since the first brush stroke is parallel to the join, it is possible to dip twice, once for each side. Try to make the first brush strokes on each side in a slightly different place for each coat. The back may be varnished as stage C but, unlike with oil varnish, brush from the centre join to the edges. There it helps to hold the brush a little more upright to get more

RIGHT: Brush directions for varnishing a front with spirit varnish.

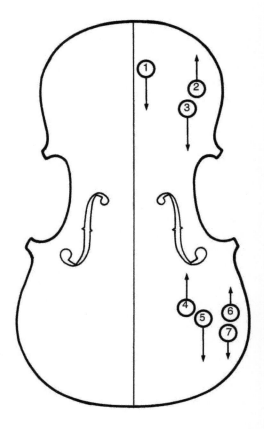

varnish into the curve. Brush with the angle of the figure. Varnish the front. When varnishing either the back or the front as shown on the right, hold the instrument either on its pin or on its scroll for alternate coats. The ribs may be varnished across or along; or the edges from the rib towards the back or the front, both putting varnish on where it is needed and removing that which has spread on to the edges from the main surface of the back and the front. The scroll should be started round the fluting beginning under the chin and then the top walls of the pegbox should be varnished across with a nearly dry brush. Use a well squeezed-out dip under the hen's tail and across the pegbox walls, following the figure and gradually spiralling round the volute to the eye. If any part of the instrument is too pale it is possible, after the coat is dry, to touch in the colour with an almost dry paint brush; but dark spots are hard to remove. Only a little rubbing down is needed between coats, with very worn, fine sandpaper dry. But finish with two or three colourless coats which can be well rubbed down and then polished (being careful at the same time not to remove varnish) with a little more varnish or benzoin polish on a piece of soft cotton rag, keeping the surface well lubricated with mineral oil so that the cloth does not stick to the varnish.

11 SETTING UP THE INSTRUMENT

As a violin cannot be set up until it is made, this chapter must necessarily come last, but it is the most important. If the fingerboard is not a normal curve and smooth the player will not be happy. If the pegs do not move smoothly and hold in place the player cannot tune the instrument, and both the soundpost and the bridge have a great influence on tone, though no one yet exactly understands in what way.

THE FINGERBOARD

The false fingerboard will be easy to remove and then the neck must be scraped clean of glue, taking care to keep the surface really flat. The gluing surface of the fingerboard must also be scraped clean. If the two surfaces do not fit perfectly, take a very sharp block plane and test the fingerboard first. If the two surfaces still do not fit, it will be necessary to plane the neck. At this stage hold the fingerboard in place and test the elevation. If it is too high, plane a very little from the root end; if it is too low, plane very little near the pegbox. While it is being planed, the neck should be supported with the underneck cramping block, which will be needed for gluing the fingerboard on to the neck. The fingerboard is easier to locate if the nut is still glued on, but there should be no glue underneath it. Warm the neck and the fingerboard, apply thin glue – if the glue is too thick the surfaces will skid about rather than gripping in place – and cramp carefully in place with the two cramping blocks only. If the root end of the fingerboard does not sit down

tightly you can put another cramp across to the button, lining the cramping block with non-stick paper or soap, but there is then a risk of marking the varnish.

When the glue is dry, hold a short piece of lining wood or something similar against the nut and give it a sharp tap. This should dislodge the nut. Put a cloth under the fingerboard to protect the body of the instrument and another cloth over the edge of the bench and check the dip in the length of the fingerboard and the curve and plane it if necessary. When both are right use a flat file up and down the fingerboard to remove any ridges. Scrape to remove file marks and then sandpaper diagonally from both sides and then up and down, taking care not to round down the ends of the fingerboard. It is safer to use the coarser sandpaper on a block. The fingerboard may then be polished with fine paper and oil and the nut reglued. The top of the nut must also be shaped. Imagine the path of the string to the peg on which it will be wound and make a slightly curved surface that follows this line. Allow for the shallow grooves in which the strings lie and leave a gap under them. Players vary in their preferences – from the thickness of a postcard to the thickness of the string. A high nut can always be lowered; a low nut is not so easy to improve. The nut grooves will be made later.

THE NECK

If you are lucky, the fingerboard width will fit the neck perfectly. If not, use a scraper cautiously and fine sandpaper and make the edges perfectly smooth. If you have used spirit varnish you can clean the neck. The edge of the varnish above the root should be shaped in a curve towards the hen's tail, beginning 20mm from the base. Under the hen's tail make a similar curve towards the root, beginning where the fingerboard and the nut meet. Stain the neck, using oil colour, and polish it with linseed oil and shellac. If, having used oil varnish, you clean and stain the neck as above, the process may leave a step at each end where the varnish stops. The oil varnish is not soluble in the shellac used for polishing but the spirit varnish is. If it does look a little untidy or not totally smooth then rub it with the Micro-Mesh and, if need be, polish it with shellac and linseed oil. The finish on the neck must be hard to withstand the wear of the player's hand. Repeated applications of linseed oil will also harden the wood.

THE SADDLE

There will have been a considerable build up of varnish on the saddle and this needs to be scraped off with a small scraper, working in from each edge. You will need to remove this varnish or the tailgut, in time, will spread the varnish from under it sideways and this will not look very attractive, and might even be sticky. Rub the saddle with soap.

THE PEGS

Pegs are usually bought part-made, but if you have a lathe you can turn your own and you will understand that making one is not too difficult, but to produce four matching ones is more taxing. English box or rosewood is the best material. It is better that the peg wears than the peghole, but, since the peghole is virtually end grain, it is harder than the shaft of the peg.

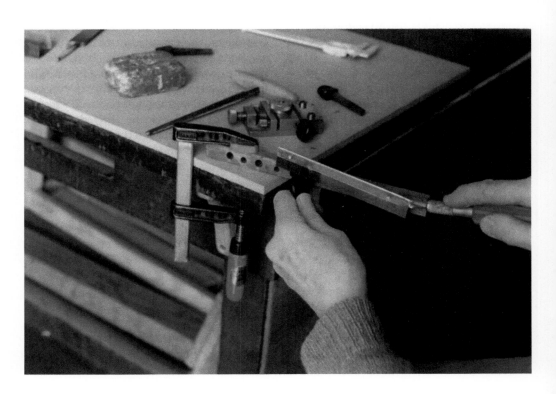

Sawing below the peg collar.

Before shaping the shaft it is as well to saw a little deeper around the collar of the peg, which, as the grain runs across it, is easily chipped.

When using the pegshaper try to take off equal amounts all the way round. If the grain does not run exactly along the shaft the pegshaper may easily remove more from one side of the peg than the other and the shaft may end up out of alignment with the head. Be particularly careful at the beginning. Unshaped pegs are often oval due to the uneven shrinkage of the wood, and so the first shavings taken are more difficult but critical. When all the pegs are nearly to the correct size, ream out the pegholes a little until the small end of the tapered shaft goes into the larger hole. Working on all four pegs, let them in further checking from on top and in front that they are parallel.

When there is still a distance of 20mm (more for cellos) between the peg collar and the pegbox, put more soap on the pegs, turn them in their pegholes and check the shine on the peg. Are both marks equally shiny? If not, you can adjust the blade of the pegshaper; but it is easier to put a sliver of sandpaper – abrasive side against the pegshaper – at the end where more wood needs to be removed. If anything, the pegs should fit more firmly in the larger hole. When the pegs fit, ream the hole gently until the collar of the peg is the correct distance from the pegbox wall. Mark with a point where the holes for the strings will come. The top peg can have its hole centrally in the pegbox; the next peg down can have its hole a similar distance from the pegbox wall; the next peg down 1mm less; and the bottom peg 1mm more. Also mark the ends of the pegs 1mm away from the outside wall of the pegbox. Ream a hole in a scrap piece of wood, hold the peg in it and drill a hole of the correct size for the string straight through the peg. While the peg is being held saw off the end on the mark, being careful not to split the wood.

These ends must now be gently domed. Put a little bevel round the edge, holding the peg at an angle to the jig and rotating it as you file. Then continue to file, holding the peg more and more upright.

Reaming peg holes.

Shaping the ends of the pegs.

BOTTOM: *Location of the holes for the strings in the pegs.*

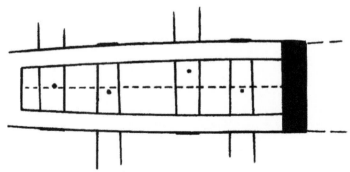

Sandpaper the end, lick it and rub it on your apron. Then rub it on the side of your nose and polish it again on your apron.

An apron is an indispensable asset when violin-making: it can be used for polishing pegs, protecting thumbs and generally keeping things clean.

THE ENDPIN

It is wise to turn down the endpin to a slightly smaller size. Then, at least, if you make the hole too big you can buy an endpin that will still fit. But if you ream the hole carefully, lining up the reamer with the centre join of the back and the rib edge, this will not be necessary.

THE SOUNDPOST

If you measure the width of the bridge feet, a normal position for the soundpost is that distance behind the bridge (towards the tailpiece) in line with the middle of the foot of the bridge. With your thumb tucked behind your apron, cut one end of the soundpost to a slight angle so that the end grain of the soundpost will be at right angles to the grain of the front. Put it through the top hole of the f and mark on the soundpost where the outside of the front comes. If the soundpost will not go through the hole use a thinner piece of wood. This gives you the approximate length of the soundpost, so you can now cut it 1mm longer and bevel the top end. Theoretically, the ends should be domed, but the curvature of the back and the front is so slight that a flat surface will fit.

Sharpen the soundpost setter to a fine edge like a chisel and impale the soundpost on the end at such an angle that it will be upright when the soundpost setter is withdrawn through the f-hole. Look in through the endpin hole and check that the soundpost is upright. If it is not, gently push and pull it with the other end of the soundpost setter until it is, keeping the slot made by the soundpost setter facing the f-hole. If the soundpost fits well it will not pivot if tapped sideways. It will probably fall over many times and you will learn to shake the instrument so that the soundpost lodges in the length of the f-hole and can be removed. Cello soundposts may be caught with a grab used by makers of electronic equipment.

This is a saying of one of my pupils: 'I have realized when making instruments that one must be impatient at first and progressively more patient as the work continues.' At no time is this dictum more true.

Check the fit of the soundpost with a dental mirror and check its position with a strip of thin plastic with a slit in it. Setting a soundpost is not easy, although it becomes more so with practice. After a few months the soundpost will be too short, because the tension of the strings will slightly distort the body, therefore a longer one will be needed.

THE BRIDGE

It is worth buying a good quality bridge blank; both the wood and the design are important. If you have a choice, look at the sides of the bridges and choose one with the medullary rays running up the center, not angled across. Begin by flattening the back – the side nearer the tailpiece – of the bridge. This should be the side to which the medullary rays are most nearly

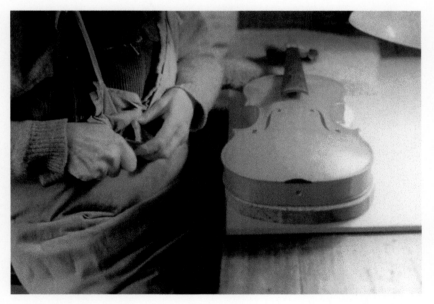

parallel. The feet of the bridge must fit the arching of the front. First mark the position of the bridge by using a chinagraph pencil or small squares of not very sticky label material. Imagine a line joining the inside f-nicks. Two-thirds of the bridge foot width should be in front of this line. The bridge should be equidistant from the

TOP: Setting a soundpost.

BELOW: Cutting the feet of the bridge to make them fit the front.

TOP: *Shaping the bridge, held in its cradle, with a knife.*

BELOW: *Shaping the ankles and the undercurve of the bridge.*

touch the front. (As so often, you have to remove the places that touch in order that the places which do not will do so.)

When cutting, also aim to reduce the thickness of the bridge foot so that the minimum thickness is 1.5mm, but probably only at one corner. Decide on the height of the bridge by looking down the length of the fingerboard or with rulers; it is safest to leave it a little high and then put a string in place on each side and check the string height at the end of the fingerboard, allowing for the string groove. Draw a curve of the appropriate radius, trim off some excess with a knife and then, holding the bridge flat over the edge of the bench, smooth the top with sandpaper held tightly round an old wooden ruler, working up and down, thus keeping the top edge square to the back. Bevel the top of the bridge to the correct thickness, working only on the side nearer the fingerboard, and check the width of the feet. It now helps to groove a block of wood so that the bridge can be held in the groove. Cutting with the grain from the centre outwards, shape the bridge so that it curves from side to side, curves slightly from the centre between its ankles to the top, but has straight sides.

Smooth this surface and then, choosing a knife blade with a long point, shape the curve under the centre to a low ellipse and the curves outside the ankles to a C shape. This should make all the ends of the feet 1.5mm thick.

With dividers set to the distance between the strings, mark four points equidistant from the outside edges and use the dividers to make a scratch mark across the top thickness of the bridge. The nut grooves may be marked in a similar way, scratching only from the edge of the nut nearest the fingerboard back towards the pegbox. With a small, round needlefile, make smooth grooves the depth of half the thickness of the

f-holes. If, after the bridge has been fitted, the back of the bridge is at right angles to the line where the ribs and front meet, the top of the bridge will be above the line joining the f-nicks, thus giving the correct stop length. Cut the feet of the bridge from the outside edge towards the centre, deciding where to remove wood by sitting the bridge in place and noticing which places

string on the bridge. At the nut the depth may be less, but must leave the desired height above the fingerboard. Think of the angle of the strings and slightly curve all the grooves to follow their line.

THE TAILPIECE

If the instrument is to be played by a child or a beginner, a tailpiece with four built-in adjusters is best. Adding four metal adjusters to a wooden tailpiece increases the weight so much that it will act as a mute. A tailpiece that is too light will cause an uneven response from the four strings, but this is unlikely. Adjust the tailpiece fastener to be so short that the tailpiece goes only just over the saddle – they always stretch – and trim off the ends. Rub a little soap on the saddle.

THE STRINGS

There are strings with a gut core, strings with a nylon core and strings entirely made from metal. Gut is an ideal material as it is not too stiff and has very good damping properties. One note should not go on resonating when the player has moved on to the next. Nylon strings have been greatly improved, although they still feel harder under the player's fingers. Metal strings are made in many ways with multiple cores and extra casing, but the majority are still stiffer, causing the harmonics that enhance each note to be sharp and musicians may find this painful. A violin E string is now always metal, unless on a violin set up as baroque, and, since the ear cannot hear the high harmonics of notes on the E string, this does not cause problems. Gut strings are not made to be used in tailpieces with adjusters; they are easier to adjust with the pegs.

Whichever strings are chosen, begin by tensioning the highest and the lowest, having first lubricated the string grooves with soap or graphite.

Check that the bridge remains upright; it will need to be straightened.

Having pushed the string just through the hole in the peg, put one turn on the far side from the peghead and all the rest between the hole and the pegbox wall nearest the peghead.

Sometimes with small instruments there

TOP: Stringing the violin.

BELOW: Straightening the bridge.

The strings are wound towards the peg head.

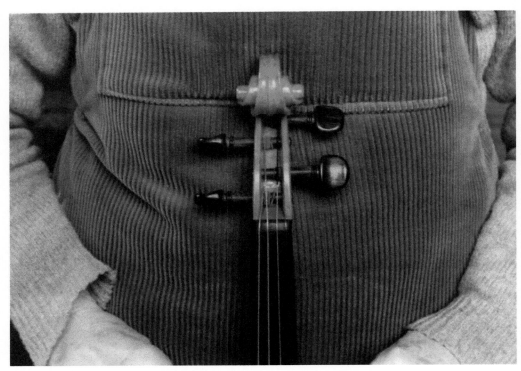

is too long a string end and therefore a danger of forcing the peg into the pegbox. If this seems to be the case, cut the end of the string off, but, if you are making a small instrument, always buy strings made for that size. They are available. When fitting a chinrest, if the varnish is at all soft, put chalk on the surfaces touching the varnish. Rather than buy a chinrest you can make one and buy the fittings. Pearwood is especially suitable.

PLAYING

When first playing the instrument I hope that you will be pleased with its tone, but do not act rashly if you are not. If the instrument shrieks it may help to make the bridge more flexible by enlarging the holes. If it is woolly it may help to move the soundpost closer to the bridge. A soundpost pulled tightly towards the f-hole may make the instrument brighter and louder, though it is not good for the instrument in the long run. Theoretically, a longer soundpost or one further from the bridge improves the lower strings, but, best of all, leave the instrument as it is. More than once, instruments that have disappointed me or been difficult to play at first have developed into ones I liked especially. If you have found the fitting of a bridge and soundpost an almost insoluble difficulty, there should be a professional violin-maker in your area who will undertake the job for you. This could well improve the tone of your instrument. Violin-makers, who also repair, do this job often and so have much more experience.

Players and instruments have to match. Some players spend all their lives looking for the perfect instrument; others happily make any instrument respond and produce the tone they want and you must find a player who enjoys playing your instrument, or best of all, play it yourself.

12 THE BAROQUE VIOLIN

'Baroque' is a term applied by musicians to music written between approximately 1650 and 1750, followed by classical music from 1750 to 1850 and romantic from then until the twentieth century. As musicians were their customers, to be pleased, violin-makers were encouraged to experiment and any so-called improvements they made are the result of the wishes of musicians. The fiddles made before the time of Andrea Amati may have been louder and suitable for playing dance music but his instruments were made for music to be listened to and have quality of tone. Since then the necks have been made longer and thinner to facilitate shifting, bridges are higher and more curved, and violins have been modified to produce a more powerful tone. The amazing fact is that the violins made earlier were capable, with these alterations, to withstand the greater pressures and still vibrate well.

The change in the design of the bow from out-curved to in-curved, perfected by Tourte in the last quarter of the eighteenth century, was the catalyst, so, to be correct, the model of a maker who worked before this period should be taken when making a baroque violin. Since this easily includes Stradivarius, all the Guarnerius family, Stainer and all the Amatis, there is no lack of good models. If the potential player also plays a modern set-up violin, a long-pattern Stradivarius is quite a good choice since, even though the proportions of the neck to the body stop can be as in the majority of baroque instruments, the full string length will be similar to that on a modern violin.

No-one knows what baroque tone was like and musicians may well have wanted, even centuries ago, to play louder than their neighbour, let alone louder than the brass and the wind. Due to the use of a baroque bow, the string will vibrate more immediately and more clearly. If the instrument has gut strings, a lower angled neck, a thinner bridge supported on a shorter bass-bar and a thinner soundpost it should have a clear tone.

To make an authentic baroque violin the modern maker, having chosen his model, should research the working methods of this maker, the materials he used and, more particularly, the tools. In this way it is possible to reproduce truly a given style. However, for those who just want a baroque violin, it is also possible to choose a model and follow the working methods of an imaginary sixteenth-, seventeenth- or eighteenth-century instrument maker who has seen, say, a Stainer violin. He would have used the techniques he knew and might have let the ribs into a groove in the back, as was sometimes done in the Low Countries and Switzerland, where they also made scroll, neck and top block from one piece of wood, a method also used in eastern Europe. For convenience, today's maker could use today's techniques for most of the process and change only a few details. Whatever method is chosen, the likelihood is that some maker, sometime, somewhere will have already done it.

Nor can anyone put a date to exactly when a certain change was made. By the time the new style of bow had been introduced, Paris had become the centre of musical development rather than Italy, so it is most likely there that new longer necks were first grafted on to violins and bass-bars were fitted under tension. However there are twentieth-century violins which, even though crudely made, have short, fat necks. The scroll, neck and top-blocks are all made from one piece of wood with the top ribs wedged in. They are certainly not classical baroque violins but neither are they modern ones. They would have been made without a mould, with the ribs built up on the back. We shall reject that method and the use of an outside mould and keep to an inside mould.

THE BODY

The ribs may be made exactly as for a modern violin and so may the back and the front, except that the purfling in the front should also be laid in with no gaps at the top and the bottom, as neither the neck nor the saddle will cut through the purfling. Even the f-hole may be cut as usual, but the bass-bar will be different.

As the bridge is lower, the pressure down on the front is less and there is no need to fit the bass-bar so that it pushes up under the bridge. It should be fitted exactly to the curve of the front, with no spring. The length of the bass-bars in the violins of Stradivarius varied from 255 to 240mm, though some of the even earlier makers fitted longer bars as well as shorter ones. They all had very tapered ends and the height was much lower and the thickness less. An average thickness was 4.5mm with a height of 8mm maximum. Even at the beginning of the twentieth century in France, Tolbecque, who wrote an entertaining book on violin-making, quotes a length for a bass-bar of ten thumbs and six lines, equal to 267mm, as is usual today, but with a thickness of 4.25mm and a height of 10.6mm, both less than is now usual. However, the Hills in their book on Stradivarius published at the same time give the modern bar a thickness of 6.3mm, really sturdy, and a height of 11.1mm. All violin-makers have their own ideas. Whatever the length, thickness and height chosen, the bar should be well-rounded right to the ends which taper down to nothing.

The next decision to make is whether to glue on the front before setting the neck. For those who have previously made violins in this way it is easier to end up with the fingerboard correctly aligned and the desired elevation if the neck is set into a completed body.

THE SCROLL

The scroll may be made as usual, but when it is sawn out the neck should be left thicker and the distance between the hen's

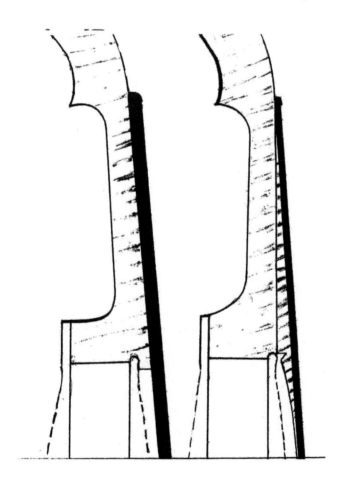

Modern and baroque necks and fingerboards set at the appropriate angle in the body.

tail and the button must be smaller. The head of the scroll pattern should be set 2mm back from the line of the surface to which the wedge and the fingerboard will be glued.

However, as this line will end up as a continuation of the line of the edge of the front, rather than being raised 7mm above the front and angled back, the eye of the scroll will not lie on a line following up from the edge of the back, as on a modern violin, but will be further forwards.

THE FINGERBOARD

The length of an early fingerboard varied between 190 and 250mm, but was wider, between 27 and even 30mm at the top and 38 to 43mm at the lower end. Sadly, the lower end of the pegbox of many early instruments has been narrowed in to the width of a modern fingerboard. Early fingerboards were often made from maple, sometimes inlaid with patterns in ivory and ebony or were veneered with ebony. Gluing even thin ebony veneer to a curved surface is not easy and so a simple solution

is to glue a flat piece of ebony on to maple and shape the top of the ebony into a curve with a radius of 52mm, leaving only 1mm of thickness on the edges. The difference will be obvious only at the wide end of the fingerboard where the undersurface should be hollowed as a modern fingerboard is and the advantage is that, when the fingerboard has grooves in it from the strings and the player's fingers, it can be planed smooth again several times.

The wedge may be made either from maple or ebony. If it is made from maple it should be cut on the quarter, preferably with the grain following the grain of the neck. If it is made from ebony it is not so important whether it is cut on the quarter or not. The wedge should be glued to the fingerboard. Then the wedge is planed to produce a combined thickness of the wedge and the fingerboard of 4mm at the top and 18mm at the end of the neck. The elevation should then be correct, given a neck stop of 126mm or so. If the neck stop is longer the thickness must be a little greater at the end of the neck, though, again, these measurements will have

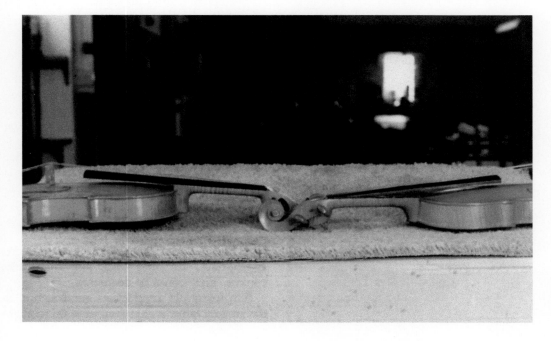

The contrast between modern and baroque necks.

ABOVE: Template for a baroque neck.

ABOVE RIGHT: Design for a bridge after Stradivarius.

BELOW: Baroque and modern tailguts.

varied greatly and the bridge height will not always have been 29mm.

PREPARING TO SET THE NECK

First the root of the neck must be cut to length and the shaping made at the end of the wedge as follows. The root may be cut to the neck stop length plus 3.5mm and at an angle of 93 degrees, rather than the 87-degrees angle suggested for modern violins. In this way if the rib is only just cut on the front edge and the fingerboard surface of the neck follows the line of the edge of the front, the neck will be let in deeper at the button. The wedge-shape of the sides of the neck will ensure that the

neck root sits well down on the top block and it will be therefore much easier to glue in. Where the cut up into the wedge comes can vary, but it looks better if it lines up with the top edge of the front. After a V cut, the underneath of the wedge should curve up elegantly to the end of the fingerboard. When this has been done and the root of the neck planed smooth, the wedge can be temporarily glued to the neck.

When shaping the sides of the neck and the fingerboard, make the sides of the fingerboard and the wedge only slightly tapered and then make the sides of the neck more definitely tapered from the wedge to the width where the button will come, leaving extra wood beyond this point if possible.

Using a lower elevation stick, follow the instructions for setting the neck.

SHAPING THE NECK

The combined thickness of the neck, the wedge and the fingerboard should be 21mm under the hen's tail and increase to 30mm above the button. The curve at both ends should follow the template and the rounding should be semi-circular.

THE SADDLE

Cut a recess in the front the length of the saddle, which is slightly shorter than usual, and half the thickness of the edge. The saddle is a piece of hardwood or bone replacing the spruce, which is so soft that it would quickly be worn into groves under the tailgut. Due to the way the tailgut is fitted, the saddle is no higher than the edge.

FITTINGS

Peg heads with flat sides seem more appropriate, or ones that are slightly convex. They could be decorated.

Not many old soundposts survive, but the general belief is that they were thinner.

The placing of them was probably similar to today's practice. Bridge designs were also various. The one shown comes from a design by Stradivarius, which is beautiful.

The feet were probably 4mm thick and the top thickness 1.5mm. The top curve should follow the fingerboard and the string heights above the fingerboard will be lower the shorter the fingerboard is. The string spacing may be wider at the nut, up to 6mm, but as on a modern violin at the bridge.

Tailpieces were simple in outline and lighter than modern ones. An average length was 100mm, with a width of 38mm at the top, curving in gently to one of 18mm at the end. The four holes for the strings should have centres 8mm apart and the holes should be small, 3mm in diameter, and there is no bar for the strings to rest on. At the end near the saddle the holes, drilled in the same way, also have centres 8mm apart and their diameter should be similar to that of the tying gut to be used, perhaps an old double bass string. The advantage of real gut is that if, after calculating the length, the ends are put in a flame and then pushed against the bench, a stop is formed and a simple half-hitch will hold the tailpiece in place. Have faith, and perhaps an extra pair of hands to hold the knot in place while the strings are brought up to tension. Strings specifically made for baroque instruments are now made by several firms and are easily obtained.

The term 'classical violin' may be applied to any instrument somewhere in design between a baroque and a modern violin. At any one time many sorts of violin were being made and to categorise them is as difficult as separating folk fiddles from violins.

13 FOLK FIDDLES

ABOVE: Original instruments made in a camp for refugees from El Salvador.

Making a bass in the refugee camp.

The first years of the twenty-first century could be a turning point in the history of the fiddle. For years players wanted a 'proper' violin, but now the traditional instruments are being reintroduced and remaining examples are cherished even if they were quite roughly made. Fiddles evolved in parallel with violins from the same roots or just from man's instinct to make music from amplified strings. The first makers of the Welsh crwth or the Shetland gue simply made boxes with taut strings on top and had probably never seen anything resembling a rebec. People in countries well distant from each other also solved problems in the same way. Fitting a sound-post is tricky and so the Greek lira, the Polish mazanki and the crwth all have a bridge with one short leg and one much longer leg that passes through a hole in the front of the instrument and rests on the back.

Much later the makers of the Hardanger fiddles must have seen German violins, which they resembled closely, before they developed into the decorated instruments with distinctive f-holes that they now are. They were first made at the beginning of the seventeenth century, and at that time were smaller and had only two or three sympathetic strings. It was also at this time that decorated instruments were made in the Black Forest and Switzerland, although they were intended for playing classical as well as folk music. Whittling and decorating are good occupations for isolated communities during long winter evenings and if you had no instrument and wanted to play for the dances in the summer, making one would be a sensible thing to do.

The violin family have long been adopted in South America. Even in a camp for refugees from El Salvador wonderful instruments are now made. Cortez took musicians with him and the early missionaries were encouraged to teach music to make themselves accepted. This is in contrast to the attitude of religious leaders in Shetland, Hungary and other countries where the violin was regarded as an instrument of the devil to be discouraged and destroyed if possible.

Violins went to North America with the early settlers and there are great similarities between the folk tunes of the old world and of the new, for example, between those of Shetland and Newfoundland. American folk music has many roots, from the slaves and the settlers, and continues still to evolve. Today most fiddlers there and in England play on standard violins but set up with metal strings and a flatter bridge since they often want to bow two strings at once. Some use electric violins but, since they usually have solid bodies and are amplified, they fit in better with electronic instruments than with violin-making.

From eastern Europe the violin moved yet further east and gradually displaced the local instruments or joined in with them. In India a violin is held with the scroll against the seated player's foot. In China a two-string fiddle is played with the bow threaded between the strings and held with the endpin downwards. In Hungary the accompanying fiddle is held on the shoulder but with the front of the instrument at right-angles to the floor. Upright, upside down or sideways, they are all fiddles and the varieties to copy are innumerable.

THE HARDANGER

The one instrument that has developed in a way interesting to the violin-maker is the Hardanger fiddle and so a description of the differences follows. Outlines vary, a classical model may be followed or an outline from a seventeenth- or an eighteenth-century German violin. Modern Hardangers often have a longer upper and lower bout and shorter C-curve. The overall length is 7mm greater but the body stop remains 195mm. The differences begin when making the front, the neck, the scroll, the fingerboard and the bridge.

The front can be sawn out and the arching planed to height as usual but, as the area between the f-holes is almost flat, it is wise to draw on the f-holes already. The distance between the top holes is 38mm and the distance from the finished edge to the lower hole about 15mm, although this will depend on the model chosen. The main stem of the f-hole should be parallel to the centre join of the front. The arching curve can then be gouged towards the end blocks from where

LEFT: A modern Hardanger violin made by Evan Turner.

Template drawings for the
Hardanger drawn on
10mm squares.

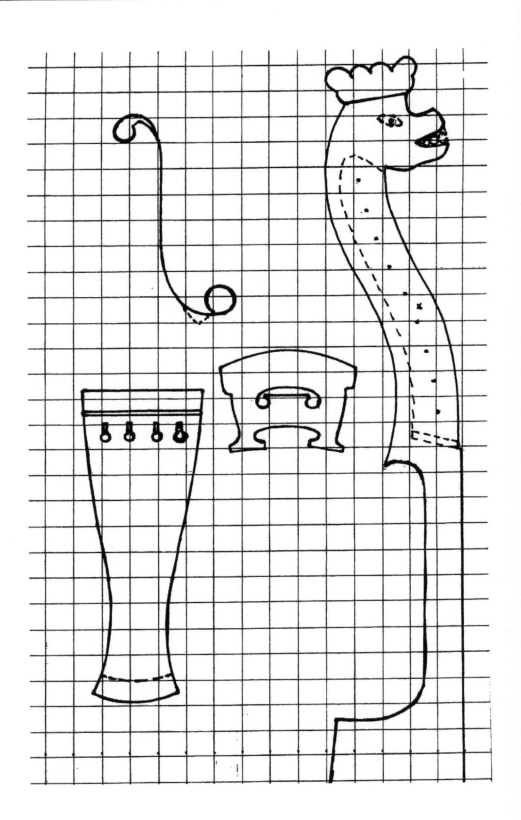

the f-holes end. In the C-curve gouge the edges down nearly to thickness but leave the area around the f-holes intact. The edges can now be thicknessed and the back and the front temporarily glued to the ribs and the outline trimmed. A decorative inlay can then be fitted instead of purfling, but the gouging next to the edge will be less marked and done with a shallower gouge. The cylindrical area between the f-holes can now be planed to a flattish cylinder, leaving the height of 16.5mm along the join, curving down at each side to13mm along the stem of the f-hole. This can easily be measured with a pencil calliper. The arching can also be planed smooth down towards the end blocks. This area and the cylinder can be scraped smooth and the f-holes redrawn. With a pencil calliper set to 13mm, draw a line on the inside of the front the complete length of the f-holes plus 10mm at the lower end, and mark the areas from these lines outwards to the edges. Also mark the areas for the top and the bottom blocks and the gluing area for the ribs and linings. These are the areas not to be gouged. Reset the pencil calliper to 5mm and gouge the remaining area of the front to that thickness and then plane to 3.5mm.

F-HOLES

On the outside of the front put soft pencil marks dividing the f-hole into four equal parts. Cut down with a knife along the two central parts at right-angles to the flat side of the front and gouge away the edge of the front. Continue alternately cutting and gouging until a thickness of 5mm remains. This should make a wall on the f-hole line

7mm from the top of the arching down to the continuation of the edge thickness. Leave a thickness of 3mm at the top of the wall and below it drill five 3mm holes parallel to the flat side of the arching, through into the central area of the front that has been hollowed out. These holes can then be joined up with a knife and an unattached hacksaw blade.

It is wise first to try cutting an f-hole in a spare piece of wood shaped like the arching.

With this opening made it is now possible to finish the arching. The arching drops steeply from the central cylinder to the corners, but there is no sudden step down from the top hole of the f nor below the lower hole, only in the centre of the f-hole where the gap is 5mm from top to bottom, big enough for the soundpost to pass through.

A fretsaw can now be threaded through and the top curve and the top hole sawn out. Only the lower hole should then be cut out and not joined up to the central hole. With a hacksaw blade held parallel to the flat side of the front, the central hole can be extended towards the lower hole, leaving a thickness of 3mm both above

BELOW: A trial f-hole with a hack-saw blade in place.

LEFT: The central cross-section of the f-hole.

A completed f-hole.

and below the cut, which diminishes to a height of 2mm as it meets the lower hole. The lower wing of the f-hole which extends inside the instrument can now be shaped, mainly working from the inside of the arching. After this has been done, the thickness of the front may be planed and scraped down to 3mm and a baroque style bass-bar fitted. A modern-style saddle should be fitted and then, after the linings are glued in and the blocks and linings shaped, the front can be glued on.

THE SCROLL

Modern Hardangers are made with four or five sympathetic strings and so the pegbox must be long. It is finished, not with a scroll, but a head, usually that of a dragon with a crown on. A long tongue or a burst of flame may be added to its mouth. Half-size violin pegs should be used with the centres 12mm apart. The holes should be drilled while the sides of the neck-block are still square.

THE FINGERBOARD

The fingerboard is made from ebony and is 235mm long, 24mm wide at the top and 44mm at the lower end. The curve is the same as on a baroque violin, with a radius of 52mm. Underneath there must be a central groove 3mm deep and 10mm wide at the top, increasing to 20mm at a point 136mm from the top and continuing to the end, which may be further hollowed out as a modern violin fingerboard is. The neck should be cut to a length of 136mm and at an angle of 87 degrees at the root. It has a similar groove to the fingerboard. Where the groove meets the pegbox, fit a hard wood insert in the pegbox 3mm wide, with grooves for the sympathetic strings to rest in. If a 2mm-pin is put across the pegbox between the fourth and the fifth peghole, 6mm down from the top edge, the sympathetic strings can pass over this, rather than rest on the pegs of the four main strings.

THE NECK

The temporary gluing of the fingerboard to the neck must be done with the minimum amount of glue as the surfaces each side of the groove are narrow and fragile. When the glue is dry, the root of the neck can be shaped as on a modern violin and the recess cut for the neck. The elevation should be 26mm to give a bridge height of 31mm. The neck shaping and the fitting of the pegs and the soundpost are as on a modern violin although, since the top of the soundpost is so flat, they are not so easy to fit.

THE BRIDGE

A special bridge must either be bought or made, following the pattern. Enough must be cut off the feet when the bridge is fitted to leave the bar for the sympathetic strings 20mm above the arching curve. The top of the bridge should be cut to a radius of 55mm or even flatter. The top thickness is normal, as are the string spacings at both the bridge and the nut.

THE TAILPIECE

The tailpiece is heavier than normal. The outline is given and the curvature should be the same as that of the top of the bridge. The thickness at the bridge end is 5mm right across the curve and at the narrow end it is flat underneath and 7mm thick. It has a bar for the strings to pass over, as on a modern tailpiece, and the hole for the top string, which will have an adjuster, is of the usual size, but the other three are often smaller. All the string holes have a slit extending towards the bar. Evan Turner's tip for fitting the two hooks for the sympathetic strings under the tailpiece is as follows: drill two 2mm-holes 10mm apart through the groove that has to be made to take the bar and thread wire through the holes before gluing the bar in place and shaping it. The wire may then be bent to come out forwards and back to make the hooks. Nowadays the tailpiece has holes to take the tailpiece fastener drilled through parallel to the flat side, with recesses on each side, like a modern tailpiece; however, it could also be attached like a baroque tailpiece and the saddle lowered.

DECORATION

Traditionally, both the fingerboard and the tailpiece, and sometimes also the pegheads are inlaid with geometric patterns in mother-of-pearl. The body of the instrument is decorated with baroque curlicues, often ending in the shapes of leaves or stylized flowers, drawn or painted on in black. The early Hardangers were less decorated.

If you are making a violin specifically for folk music there is no reason why it too cannot be decorated. With imagination, an original instrument can be made and, by using silk dyes, applied after the sealer, any colour is possible and the main varnish can be colourless.

LEFT: A Hardanger pegbox and original head.

14 SMALL INSTRUMENTS

Many of the great makers of the past made small violins, including Stradivarius and Guarnerius del Gesu. Probably many more were made that have not survived the ravages of young players. In the nineteenth century elegant little instruments were made in Mirecourt, Mittenwald and elsewhere. Today the standard of living for makers has risen and the numerous cheap instruments that are imported make parents think twice before spending even as much, comparatively, as they would have done a century ago. However, the modern, mass-produced instruments are heavy and ungrateful to play and even a less skilled maker can make a far better instrument.

MATERIALS

Wood should be chosen that is not stiff and is as lightweight as possible. For the back and the ribs a good choice is alder, slab-sawn maple, lime, poplar or fruit wood. These woods are also possible for the neck and the scroll but great care must be taken to chose wood sawn on the quarter and with straight grain. The blocks and linings can be made from pencil cedar (which is light though not very easy to bend), yellow pine or light spruce. These woods may also be used for the front and so may sitka spruce. As the specific gravity of wood varies from tree to tree it is best to feel the planks and choose the lightest and softest.

DESIGN

The shape of the children must be taken into account as well as their ideas of what an instrument should look like. The length of the arm is less, proportionally to the body, in small children and, in particular, the ribs of small cellos need to be low if the player is going to be able to bow and finger at the same time. Higher ribs make a very small difference to the body resonances of instruments and, as recent research on violas – which share many of the problems of small violins – shows that low ribs produce better tone on the low strings, it is probably better to make all small instruments with lower ribs. In the design of the outline it must be remembered that even small players may want to shift to higher positions or play harmonics, so the treble shoulder must not be too square nor too wide. The C-curve, however, may be up to 5mm wider than a size proportional to a full-size violin and so may the lower bouts, although the lower corners must not stick out too far. The top corners may be dispensed with, but one set of corner blocks will give stability to the arching and also the lower corners will help to resist the pressure of the bridge.

The scroll may be lightened by using a simpler design with a hole instead of a volute. Instead of allowing for the full width for the eye of the scroll, the maximum width of the scroll block need be only slightly wider than the width of the root of the neck. Use the neck template as normal, place the centre of the hole so that the hole will come down to the throat of the neck, and the remaining wood increases in width from that point around to the pegbox. After this large hole has been drilled the scroll can be sawn out without any danger of chipping the corners. The scroll can then be made as

LEFT AND BELOW LEFT:
Simplified scroll for a
small instrument.

easier to bend. All other ribs should be 1mm as usual. The instrument must be robust enough to withstand the sometimes unpredictable actions of little players and yet, to make a better sound, it must be thinner. The front of an eighth-size violin can be reduced to 2mm, a quarter-size to 2.1mm, a half-size to 2.2mm and a three-quarters-size to 2.4mm. There is not much hope of reaching tap-tones of F or F#, although a half-size violin front can be made to within a semitone, and it is better to aim for a ringing note. A quarter-size cello made with a front 3.5mm thick has a tap-tone of E and so far has survived, although small cellos are more vulnerable.

VIOLAS

Until recently no one was interested in small violas but there is now a demand for them. Small violins with f-holes set well apart and thin fronts can work well as violas, especially if fitted with a bridge a size larger than the instrument. Experiments have recently been made to make cheap factory instruments sound more like violas. A hole is drilled under the bridge on the treble side and the bridge foot is supported on a long soundpost above the front of the instrument, leaving the whole

usual. The peg-box on small instruments should be made proportionally longer, allowing greater spacing between the pegs which may be turned an adult hand. Cutting away the back of the pegbox reduces the weight a little more and is slightly quicker to make.

THICKNESS

If the small violin has a C-curve, the ribs for it may be made as thin as 0.8mm. They are unlikely to be damaged, the curve gives them added strength and they will be

A short, broad viola.

front free to vibrate without the pivot point of the soundpost. Although this diminishes the tone of the upper strings, a relief on some cheap instruments, it does improve the tone of the lower strings. It is, however, vandalism: no good violin-maker could do this. It must never be done on a handmade instrument.

A viola with a body length of 335mm can have body widths 6 per cent wider than the figures given in the tables in Appendix I, except on the treble side of the top bout, rib heights of 27 to 29mm and arching heights of 14.5 and 15.5mm. However, use a full-size f-hole pattern and make the f-holes long and narrow, but with big nicks so that the soundpost will pass through. The body stop will be about 186mm, but, so long as the neck stop is in proportion, the exact length is unimportant. Violas are more variable in outline than most other instruments and short, broad ones with good curves can

look pleasing and, if the elevation is made 1mm higher than usual, bowing is no problem.

CELLOS

Small cellos are easier to make successfully than small violins or small violas, and the same suggestions apply: flexible wood, lower ribs and everything as lightweight as possible. They are as prone to wolf notes as full-size cellos, although these are less if a small area of the front below the bass f-hole about a third of the way down towards the lower edge is left 0.5mm thicker.

FINGERBOARDS

The lengths given in the tables (Appendix I) are aesthetically pleasing, but, since small players are unlikely to want to play high notes, fingerboards may be shorter. This will make the fingerboard lighter and every gram less helps. They must not be too thick or a comfortable neck thickness will leave too little neck and too much fingerboard. The underneath of the wide end of the fingerboard may also be hollowed further towards the neck root and along the edges.

FITTINGS

Modern pegs are large and so it is better to buy them a size smaller than the nominal size of the instrument being made. If the pegshaper is too big, strips of sandpaper may be put in, as already described. It should be possible to use the same reamer, although especially small ones are made. Bridges for small instruments should be left thicker than usual at the top curve, but the various holes can be enlarged since this improves the flexibility of the bridge and helps to eliminate high frequencies. It also makes the bridge more likely to break if the instrument is knocked, but this is preferable to cracks being made in the front. Tailpieces with built-in adjusters are made in all sizes and it should be possible, with some adjustment to the tailpiece-fastener, to achieve a length of string between the tailpiece and the bridge slightly longer than one-sixth of the vibrating string length. Changing this length may sometimes help to eliminate wolf-notes. The other great improvement for small instruments is that strings are now also made for all sizes of instrument. It is important to buy the correct length needed – which leads to the last problem of small instruments.

NOMENCLATURE

To use fractions as names for the several sizes of instrument is most confusing since there are no fixed sizes and the fractions have no exact or proportional meaning. Who knows where a quarter ends and a half begins? It is sad that inches should no longer be used since the length of the back of an instrument in inches gives a reasonable set of numbers from 9 for a one-sixth-size violin to 30 for a full-size cello. Violas are often referred to as 15½in, 16in and so on, and this gives a good idea of what size they are. Even centimetres would work quite well, with a one-sixth-size violin being called a 23 and a full-size cello a 76. It is difficult to change something that is so established, but at the beginning of a new century we could try and maybe in only another hundred years it might be accepted.

The violin family should go on to the end of time and, making instruments that last, is not only a joyful occupation but also a tiny speck of immortality in an ever-expanding universe, and even if you make only one it should still be treasured by future generations.

TAILPIECE

Appendix I

MEASUREMENTS FOR THE VIOLIN, THE VIOLA AND THE CELLO

[All measurements are in millimetres]

A. Average Measurements for Violins

		1/4	1/2	3/4	7/8	4/4
Body length		275	320	335	345	355
Body widths	upper:	139	145	156	162	167
	middle:	95	98	105	109	112
	lower:	168	182	195	202	208
Rib heights		24/26	26/28	28/30	29/31	30/32
Arching height back		12	13	14	14.5	15
	front	13.5	14	15	15.5	16
Thickness of edges	back	3	3.2	3.4	3.6	3.7
	front	3.1	3.3	3.5	3.8	4
	[0.3 thicker round middle bout and button]					
Purfling in from edge		3	3	3	3.5	4
Length of f-holes measured diagonally		66	68	71	73	75
Distance between top holes of ffs		34	36	38	41	42
Distance of ffs from outside edge		10	10	11	11.5	12
Top edge to nut ('neck stop')		98	114	122	126	130
Top edge to f-nicks ('body stop')*		147	171	183	189	195
Linings	thickness	2.0	2.0	2.0	2.0	2.1
	height	6	7	7	7	8
Bass-bar	thickness	4	4.5	4.5	5	5.5
	height in middle	9	9.5	10	11	12
Fingerboard	length	205	240	255	265	270
	edge thickness	4	4	4.5	5	5.5
	width top	21	22	23	23.5	24
	width bottom	35	37	39	42	43
	radius of curve	35	36	38	40	41
Pegbox external width at nut		21.5	22.5	23.5	24	24.5
	at top	18	18	19	20	20

Violins (continued)

	1/4	1/2	3/4	7/8	4/4
Distance between centres of pegholes (full size 15-22-15)					
Scroll width top	9	10	11	11.5	12
Pegbox width at back	22.5	23	24	24.5	25
Maximum width at eyes	38	39	40	41	42
Chin	20	21	22	23	24
Height of fingerboard line at bridge (elevation)	22	23	25	26	27
Foot of neck: fingerboard to table	5	5.5	6	6.5	7
Button width	18	19	20	20.5	21
Button height	9.5	10	11	11.5	12
Neck thickness upper (with fingerboard)	16	17	17.5	18	18.5
lower	18	19	19.5	20	20.5
Saddle length	30	32	34	34.5	35
height above table	3.3	3.4	3.4	3.5	3.5
Wall of pegbox to peg collar	9	10	10	11	12
Diameter of peg near collar	5	5.5	6	7	7.5
Soundpost diameter	4.5	5	5.5	5.5	6
Maximum width of bridge foot					4.5
Bridge thickness at the top edge					1.5–2.0
Normal bridge height (measured on instrument)					33
Radius of top of bridge curve	35	36	38	40	41
Distance apart of strings at nut	4.6	4.8	5	5.2	5.5
at bridge	9.5	10	10.5	11	11.3
String height above fingerboard end (gut or nylon core) E					2.5
G					5

Top of bridge to tailpiece bar: slightly more than 1/6 of vibrating length.

*These measurements may be altered as long as the proportion of 2:3 is kept.

B. Approximate Measurements for Violas

			Juliet Barker models		*Brothers Amati*
Body length		398	409	420	410
Body Widths	upper:	193	196	199	198
	middle:	131	134	136	134
	lower:	240	244	247	246
Rib Heights		35/37	36/38	37/39	31.5/33.5
Arching	back	16	16.5	16.5	19.5
	front	17.5	18	18	19
Thickness of edges	back	4	4	4	4
	front	4.3	4.3	4.3	3.9
[0.3 thicker round middle bout and button]					
Purfling in from edge		4.1	4.2	4.3	4
Length of f-holes measured diagonally		89	91	93	78
Distance between ffs at top		49	50	51	50
Distance of ffs from edge		13	14	15	C:20 A:21
top edge to nut (the neck stop)		140.5	144	146.5	140 or 148
top edge to f-nicks (body stop)★		211	216	220	223
Linings	thickness	2.1	2.1	2.1	2.1
	height	8	8	8	8
Bass-bar	thickness	6	6	6.5	6
	height in middle	14	14	15	14
Fingerboard	length	290	295	308	302
	edge thickness	5.5	5.5	5.5	5.5
	width top	24.5	25	25	25
	width bottom	45	46	47	47
	radius of curvature	42	42	42	
Pegbox external width	at nut	25.5	26	26	26
	at top	19	20	20	18.5
Distances between centres of pegholes (average 18-25-18)					
Scroll width	top	13.0	14.0	14.0	12.5
Pegbox width at back		26.5	27	27	27.2
Maximum width at eyes		44	45	45	42
Chin		24	25	25	
Height of fingerboard line at the bridge (elevation)		32	32	33	

Violas (continued)

	Juliet Barker models			*Brothers Amati*
Foot of neck, fingerboard to table	8	8.5	9	
Button width	22.5	23	23	20.5
Edge to top of button	14	14.5	15	13.5
Neck thickness upper	19	19	19	19
lower	21	21	21	21
Saddle length	36	37	38	36
height above table	4	4	4	4
Wall of pegbox to peg collar	12	13	14	
Diameter of peg near collar			7.5	
Soundpost diameter	6.5	6.5	7	6.5
Maximum width of bridge foot	5			
Bridge thickness at the top	2			
Normal bridge height (measured on instrument)	39	40	41	
Radius of top of bridge curve	42	42	42	
Distance apart nut of strings at	5.8	5.8	5.8	5.8
bridge	13	13	13	13
Gut string height above fingerboard end	A 3			
	C 5			

Top of bridge to tailpiece bar: slightly more than 1/6 of vibrating length.

*These measurements may be altered as long as the proportion of 2:3 is kept.

C. Approximate Measurements for Cello

		1/4	1/2	3/4	7/8	4/4
Body length		610	655	690	720	745
Body widths:	upper	280	290	315	326	340
	middle	192	200	210	225	240
	lower	362	375	400	413	440
Rib heights	upper	91	101	112	115	120
	lower	94	104	115	119	124
Rib thickness		1.3	1.3	1.4	1.4	1.4
Arching heights	back	21	22	23	24	25
	front	23	24	25	26	27
Thickness of edges	back	4.7	4.8	4.8	5	5.2
	front	5.0	5.2	5.3	5.5	5.7
		[0.3 thicker round middle bouts and button]				
Distance of purfling from edge		4.3	4.5	4.7	5	5
f-hole length measured diagonally		117	124	129	132	140
Distance apart between ffs at top		73	80	88	89	95
Top edge to nut (neck stop)		222	238	259	270	280
Top edge to f-nicks (body stop)*		317	340	370	385	400
Linings	thickness	2.1	2.2	2.3	2.4	2.5
	height	8	9	10	11	12
Bass bar	thickness	9	9.5	10	10.5	10.7
	height in middle	20	21	23	24	25
Fingerboard	length	460	487	540	560	580
	width at nut	28	29	30	31	31.5
	width bridge end	58	59	62	63	64
	radius of curvature	40	44	48	51	53†
Peg box external widths at the nut		40	44	45	46	47
at the top end		30	30	31	31	32
Peg box length		105	110	120	130	135
Scroll	minimum top	14.5	15	16	16	17
	back peg box	42	43	44	45	46
	chin	35	36	38	39	40
	hen's tail	28	29	30	31	32
maximum width at the eyes		58	61	63	65	65+

Cellos (continued)

		1/4	1/2	3/4	7/8	4/4
Distances between centres of pegholes: (full size 28-43-28)						
Height of fingerboard line at bridge		66	70	75	78	80
Table to undersurface of fingerboard (at end of neck)		18	19	20	21	22
Button	width	26	27	28	29	30
	height	20	20	21	22	22
Thickness of neck	upper	25	26	27	28	28
	lower	31	32	33	34	34
Saddle	length	48	50	53	55	55
	height above front	4.5	4.5	5	5	5
From peg collar to wall of peg box		16	17	18	19	20
Diameter of peg near collar						11
Soundpost diameter		9	9.5	10	12	12
Maximum width of bridge feet						12.5
Bridge thickness at top						2
Normal bridge height (measured on instrument)		75	78	83	86	88
Radius of top of bridge curve		41	42	45	47	48
Distance between strings at nut		6.9	7.0	7.3	7.4	7.6
	at bridge	13.7	14.0	14.5	14.8	15
Height: string above fingerboard	A					5
end for gut or nylon core	C					7.5

* These measurements may be altered as long as the proportion of 7:10 is kept.

† The Romberg slopes up at 30° to the base and is 23mm long (full-size).

Appendix II

ENGLISH, ITALIAN, FRENCH AND GERMAN TERMS

English	Italian	French	German
violin	violino	violon	geige
arching	curvatura	voûte	Wölbung
back	fondo	fond	Boden
bassbar	catena	barre	Bassbalken
blocks	blochetti	tasseaux	Klotzen
bridge	ponticello	chevalet	Steg
button	nocetta	talon	Zäpfchen
chisel	scalpello	ciseau	Meissel
endpin	bottone	bouton	Knopf
f-hole	ff	F	F-loch
file	lima	lime	Feile
fingerboard	tastiera	touche	Griffbrett
fluting	sgusciatura	coulisse	Hohlkehle
front	tavola	table	Decke
gouge	scorbia	gouge	Ausstosseisen
hen's tail	linguetta	cul de poule	Schwanz
knife	cotello	canif	Schnitzer
linings	controfasce	contre-eclisses	Reifchen
linseed oil	olio di lino	huile de lin	Leinöl
mould	forma	moule	Form
neck	manico	manche	Hals
nut	capotasto	sillet d'en haute	Obersattel
peg	caviglia	cheville	Wirbel
plane	pialletti	rabot	Hobel
purfling	filliatura	filets	Einlage
reamer	svasatore	alésoir	Wirbelbohrer
ribs	fasce	éclisse	Zargen
scraper	rasiera	ratissoire	Ziehklinge
scroll	riccio	tête	Schnecke
soundpost	anima	âme	Stimmstock
square	squadre	écaire	Winkel
tailpiece	cordiera	cordier	Saitenhalte
template	modello	modèle	Schablone
turpentine	trementina	terebenthine	Terpantin
varnish	vernice	vernis	Lack
volute	chiocciola	volute	Schneckenwindung

REFERENCE SOURCES

USEFUL BOOKS: INSTRUMENTS

Beament, J., *The Violin Explained* (Oxford: Clarendon Press, 1997; paperback edn, 2000) ISBN 0-19-816739-3

Hammerl, J. and R. Hammerl, *Varnishes for Violins* (Frankfurt: Bochinsky, 1990) ISBN 3-923639-76-7

Heron-Allen, E., *Violin Making as It Was and Is* (London: Ward-Locke, 1997) ISBN 0-7063-1045-4

Hill, H.H, A.F. Hill and A.E. Hill, *Antonio Stradivari. His Life and Works* (New York: Dover, 1963). ISBN 486-20425-1

Johnson, C. and R. Courtnall, *The Art of Violin-Making* (London: Robert Hale, 1999) ISBN 0-7079-5876-4

Sacconi, F., *The Secrets of Stradivari* (Cremona: Libreria del Convegno, 1972; English translation 1979)

BOOKS: MATERIALS AND TOOLS

Kingshott, J., *Sharpening: the Complete Guide* (Lewes: Guild of Master Craftsmen, 1994) ISBN 0-946810-48-3

Lee, L., *The Complete Guide to Sharpening* (London: Batsford, 1984)ISBN 0-7134-7859-4

Lincoln, W.A., *World Woods in Colour* (New York: Macmillan, 1986)ISBN 0-02-572350-2

Meyer, R., *The Artist's Handbook of Materials and Technique* (London: Faber, 1982) ISBN 0-571-11693-0

Morey, P., *How Trees Grow* (London: Arnold, 1973) ISBN 0-7131-2385-0/9

OTHER INFORMATION SOURCES

The British Violin Making Association is open to anyone with an interest in any aspect of violins. Enquiries to Secretary@BVMA.org.uk; further information at www.BVMA.org.uk. The Strad Library produces posters with plans of classical instruments; telephone and fax: +44 (0)1371-810433

SUPPLIERS

The suppliers we use for our workshop in Cambridge in the United Kingdom are starred in the list below.

Key:

F: fittings; GT: general tools; ST: specialist tools; V: varnish: W: wood

Touchstone Tonewoods Ltd [F, ST]
        Telephone: +44 (0)1737-2210644; fax: +44 (0)1737-262748
        Website: www.touchstonetonewoods.co.uk

*N.R.I. [V]
        telephone and fax: +44 (0)161-881-8134
        email: post@nrinstruments.demon.co.uk

*David Dyke [F, W]
        telephone: +44 (0)1435-812315; fax: +44 (0)1435 813503

*Len Labram [ST]
        telephone: +44 (0)2476-348375

*Le Bois de Lutherie [W]
        telephone: +33 3-81-86-5555; fax: +33 3-81-86-5556
        email bois.lutherie@wanadoo.fr

*Heinz Kreuzer [W]
        telephone: +49 (0)8823-2495; fax: +49 (0)8823-4498

*Axminster Tools [GT]
        telephone: +44 (0)1297-33656; fax: +44 (0)1297-35242.
        email: email@axminster.co.uk

Kremer Pigment [V]
        telephone: +1 212-219-2394; fax: +1 212-219-2395
        email: Kremerinc@AOL.com and Kremer-Pigmente@t-online.de

Orcas Island Tonewoods [W]
        telephone: +1 360-376-2747; fax: +1 360-376-4080
        email: tonewoods@rockisland.com

International Violin Co. [F, ST, V, W]
        telephone: +1 410-832-2525; fax: +1 410-832-2528
        email: intviolin@AOL.com

Luthiers Mercantile [F,W]
        telephone: +1 707-433-1823; fax: +1 707-433-8802
        email: lmi@lmii.com

The Sound Post [F]
        telephone: +1 416-971-6990; fax: +1 416-597-9923

Garrett-Wade [GT]
        telephone: +1 212-807-1155; fax: +1 212-255-8552
        email: mail@garrettwade.com

INDEX